Brock sped up, passing Noelle by a full body length as he reached his long arm out and tapped the swimming pool wall almost thirty seconds before she did

Noelle came up behind him, heart hammering in her chest. If she was going to lose, it had better be to someone who was strong enough to race at their full potential.

The race had been exhilarating and she was pumped. So much so that she had completely forgotten about Brock's reward until the moment he came closer, wrapping his arm around her waist and pulling her against his chest.

"Now the winner takes the prize," he said, lowering his head until their lips were a breath apart.

His tight grip around her waist and the close proximity of their bodies felt so right. If this was always the prize, Noelle might be tempted to lose more often.

Books by A.C. Arthur

Kimani Romance

Love Me Like No Other
A Cinderella Affair
Guarding His Body
Second Chance, Baby
Defying Desire
Full House Seduction

A.C. ARTHUR,

an award-winning author, resides in Maryland with her husband and three children. She's had a love of reading, romance novels in particular, since she was a teenager, and writing was the natural next step. Determined to bring a new edge to romance, she continues to develop intriguing plots, sensual love scenes, racy characters and fresh dialogue—always keeping readers on their toes! AC loves to hear from readers via e-mail at acarthur22@yahoo.com.

FULL HOUSE
Seduction

A.C. Arthur

To Pier and Paris, you hold a very special place
in my heart.

KIMANI PRESS™

ISBN-13: 978-0-373-86127-9

FULL HOUSE SEDUCTION

PLEASE RECYCLE
THIS PRODUCT IS RECYCLABLE

Recycling programs
for this product may
not exist in your area.

www.kimanipress.com

Printed in U.S.A.

Dear Reader,

Noelle Vincent has been an essential character in the previous Donovan books. Now it's finally *her* turn to find love! Feisty, courageous and often impetuous, Noelle has come a long way since her introduction in Jade and Linc's story as the screwed up younger sister. Now that Noelle's strapped with a college degree, a high-paying, high-profile job and a killer body, Brock Remington doesn't stand a chance.

Brock, the adopted cousin of the infamous Donovan brothers, was a case to solve all by himself. With his tattered past and his solitary thoughts, he became the best candidate for Noelle's partner. Their differences draw them together, while their individual challenges ultimately seal their fate. It was an absolute pleasure getting them together.

In this story you'll also see some old favorites: Linc, Adam, Jade and Trent. Maxwell Donovan also makes another appearance and you'll be introduced to a few new members of the Donovan clan—Bailey and Brandon, Brock's twin siblings. And, as if I haven't already given you enough to think about, Sam Desdune from *Guarding His Body* has once again stepped in to help his partner, Trent, and catches the attention of Karena Lakefield. I hope you enjoy *Full House Seduction.*

Stay tuned to the Donovans as they join forces with other high-powered, strong and loyal African-American families such as the Desdunes, the Bennetts and the Lakefields of Manhattan.

Happy reading!

AC

Chapter 1

How did I get here? Noelle Vincent asked herself as she settled into the soft leather seats of the Donovan jet.

Her bags had been stowed, her laptop and briefcase were lying in the seat beside her and her temples pulsed with a budding headache.

Glancing out the window, she swallowed, then took a deep breath. She was not a fan of flying, so flying across country definitely was not on her "to do list." Her brother-in-law knew that and for some insane reason simply did not care.

"Break down your barriers," he'd told her simply. He was always saying things like that to her, giving her endless advice and motivation. "Your life would be so much fuller if you'd open yourself up to truly living it."

Noelle had thought about his words for the rest of

that evening, and in the morning had begun packing. She'd never been this far away from home before, never been this much on her own. But Linc had confidence in her. He believed she could handle this job, that she could manage his new casino on her own.

Twenty-four months ago, Linc had believed that she could learn the business of running a casino, so much so that he'd insisted she enroll at the local community college, taking business courses by day while working right beside him at the Gramercy Casino in their home-town of Las Vegas at night. When she'd graduated with her AA degree he'd promoted her, telling her that this was just the beginning. Noelle had been nervous then, too, but Linc had insisted she was going to succeed. And she had.

He'd had faith in her then, when she was nothing but a screwup, so his continued trust in her abilities now were not to be taken lightly. That's why she was on this plane, flying across country, because Linc had put her there and he expected her to, once again, succeed. She would not let him down.

Lincoln Donovan, oldest son of Beverly and Henry Donovan, whose name was like a household word in Las Vegas due to their generous charitable contributions and philanthropic work, was sexy and arrogant. He was the owner of the Gramercy Casino and married to Noelle's older sister, Jade. Linc and Jade—about two months ago—just had their first set of twins, Torian and Tamala, who were just about the cutest little girls Noelle had ever seen. The birth had been an occasion with Linc's younger brother and his fiancée, Adam and Camille; his parents; Max and Ben, the Donovan cousins; and Noelle and Linc all squeezed into Jade's birthing room. When the moment they'd all been waiting for finally came, the guests were escorted out, all except Linc, Noelle, Beverly and Henry. It had been emotional and uplifting to watch her sister bring life into the world.

And it had been heartbreaking.

No, not really heartbreaking, more like eye-opening. Here she was, Noelle Olivia Vincent, a twenty-six-year-old college graduate, still living with her big sister and still unwed, without any prospects.

And now sitting on a plane, fastening her seat belt and trying like hell to keep her breakfast in her stomach where it belonged.

How did she get here? Not on this plane per se—because she'd already answered that one—but here, at this point in her life. That question had been on her mind more and more these days.

In the immediate sense she had an answer.

Her destination was Maryland, the Eastern Shore, near a town called St. Michaels to be exact. After all the site searching she'd done in L.A. and San Francisco, Linc had decided the extension of his famous casino would be on the east coast. Most likely because his brother Trent and Trent's friend Sam Desdune had just successfully opened a private investigation firm, one on the east coast and one on the west. Linc liked the idea of having the Donovan name represented on both sides of the country, and since he had family in Maryland, that was the logical choice.

Noelle had been working for Linc at the Gramercy since she'd lost five thousand dollars in the casino and her sister, Jade, had bargained with Linc to work it off.

That little bargain had opened the door to Jade's happily ever after. The thought never failed to make Noelle smile.

Now, two years and a college degree later, Noelle was a fantastic manager; Linc had said so himself. And he had shown his confidence in her by sending her to oversee the building and opening of the Gramercy II, the new casino she still wished were going to be in L.A.

Still, in the past couple of years Noelle had learned to take new developments in stride. And where the Donovan men were concerned, there was always something new. Trent and Tia were the newest of surprises. Who would have ever thought that Trent Donovan with his military training and fanatical outlook would end up with a beautiful supermodel? Noelle certainly didn't but had to admit that after spending some time with Tia in L.A. and getting to know her, she was the perfect match for Trent. Now they were expecting a baby and planning to get married. Trent had wanted a quick ceremony, but Tia refused to steal Camille's spotlight. Camille and Adam had just been married two weeks ago. Now, Noelle presumed, Trent would finally get Tia to agree to a quickie ceremony. And they'd better let her know when so she could fly back for the festivities.

They were her family now, the Donovans and their wives, complete with their notoriety and connections. Noelle hadn't had family in a long time and didn't want to be away from them for too long.

Karena Lakefield, Noelle's best friend, even though she spent most of her time traveling the world as a buyer for her family's art museum, had insisted this was an excellent opportunity for Noelle. But Noelle knew what she really meant. It was a good time to get away from

Vegas, from Luther and the whirlwind of drama he'd inflicted on her life.

For that, Noelle would endure the long flight and the summer months on the shore. She would endure the frizzy hair she was likely to sport as a result of the humidity and salt water combined. She would handle being away from her twin nieces and her big sister and the men she'd come to know and love as brothers.

She would go to Maryland and work like hell to once again prove that she could succeed in business, even if not in love.

Time was wasting and if there was one thing Brock Remington hated, it was wasting time.

Looping his thumbs in his belt loops he stood, legs spread, jaw clenching, eyes glued to the runway. Linc said the plane should be pulling in at four-thirty. It was five minutes to five. He should have had her—the site manager—in tow and been on his way back to his house by now. Instead he was standing here in the middle of the private hangar where it seemed too many damned people mulled about, talking and laughing and generally getting on his nerves.

Brock was a loner, raised by Albert and Darla Donovan, oil tycoons and his adoptive parents, who already had fraternal twins, Brandon and Bailey. He wasn't a Donovan by blood—in his estimation the relation came only by pity. His biological parents had a tumultuous relationship at best, from their family feud to the secret marriage and finally the scandal that rocked the small Cambridge, Maryland, town where they lived. The Remingtons became known throughout the town when

Brock's father, Jure Remington, was brutally murdered and his mother, Tarine, literally lost her mind, leaving Brock a ward of the state because neither his maternal or paternal grandparents wanted anything to do with him. At ten years old, Brock was alone in the world. That is until Albert and Darla Donovan, who were friends of Brock's parents, rescued the angry and confused boy and took him to live in Texas. For that, Brock was grateful. Living with the Donovans was clearly better than having to spend his formative years in foster care.

Still, he was not a Donovan. A fact Brock was sure to remember. Always.

The moment he'd graduated high school Brock had headed to college in Maryland. And after school he'd stayed there without any fuss from Albert, who by that time was living alone in Houston because Darla had died two years prior from breast cancer. A part of Brock had wanted to go back, to stay with the man who'd been a father to him. But Albert wasn't hearing it. He told Brock he had his own life to lead and he'd think less of him if he didn't lead it. That's what Brock had always loved about Albert—he was honest and keen and did what was best for others, despite what he wanted for himself.

The sense of never truly belonging anywhere or with anyone manifested in Brock so that now, at almost thirty-two years old, he was resigned to being alone and not looking to change that situation.

Soon after college Brock opened Remington Construction with money from a trust fund that had been set up for him by his birth parents upon his birth. He'd built his home overlooking the sparkling waters of the Chesapeake Bay, just outside the small town of St. Michaels, and he was living his life just the way he wanted to.

Until today.

Lincoln Donovan was his cousin, an astutely intelligent man with a mind for business and a desire to make money. Brock could relate to both things on a baser level. He wasn't money hungry, but he lived comfortably on his trust fund and the profits from his construction company. He knew how to run a business and how to keep the money flowing in, but he was more focused on the contentment and stability that having his own brought.

Linc had given Brock a brief overview about the current manager at the Gramercy in Las Vegas. She was Linc's sister-in-law, the younger sister of his wife, Jade. She was a recent college graduate with a sharp mind and an eye for detail. She was also a spitfire with a great sense of humor. The latter didn't matter to Brock—he was only concerned with her work attributes.

"When I decided to open another casino, I knew instantly she'd be the one to run it," Linc had said in one of their many phone conferences. Since Jade's last month of the pregnancy Linc hadn't been able to travel, so he and Brock had weekly updates scheduled to go over the Gramercy II's progress.

Building this casino had definitely been a coup for Brock because his company specialized mostly in vacation homes. Brock, along with his best friend, Kent Foster, an architect of the highest caliber, set out to create a casino unlike any ever built before in the continental U.S. And after yesterday's walk-through he was proud to say they'd done a damn good job.

Now, he was waiting for the site manager, hoping his

beautifully designed and built casino wasn't about to go
through the onslaught of female scrutiny. Granted,
Kent's wife, Josette, was an interior designer and had
already been slated to work on the casino's basic design
scheme. But Brock knew Josette, had known her for
more than five years now, and they worked well together. Outside of Linc's praise, he didn't know the site
manager or how well they'd work together.

Brock was wary of strangers, outsiders from his
world. Some would say that was odd having been the
outsider all his life. All Brock knew was that his generally solitary lifestyle worked for him. The less interac-
tion he had with people he didn't know, the better.

Besides that, he didn't want anybody coming along
slowing down his progress. Linc wanted the Gramercy II
up and running by September, no later than October. He
wanted as much holiday money spent in the casino as
possible. It was already early June. If this site manager's
eye for detail meant she was prone to start fussing about
wallpapers and paints and who knew what else, then Brock
and this project were definitely in for a long summer.

"Hi. I'm Noelle Vincent. I think you're expecting me."

Brock heard the voice and snapped out of his reverie.
He'd been so focused on his thoughts, so intent on what
he didn't want this manager from the west coast to do
to his casino that he hadn't even noticed the plane had
landed. With a sharp movement he turned and was
quickly face-to-face with her.

She'd extended her hand and was smiling up at him,
obviously waiting for him to act or get lost. He chose
the former and cleared his throat. "Yes. I'm Brock Remington," he said, reaching to clasp her hand.

Damn, it was soft.

He'd been hoping that her million-watt smile and sparkling light brown eyes weren't actually as attractive as he'd first thought. But coupled with her soft hands and that sweet buttermilk complexion, he was dead wrong. His earlier projection was now corrected—this was going to be a long, *hot* summer.

Chapter 2

"Nice to meet you, Brock. Linc told me a lot about you." She adjusted her purse and a smaller bag on her right shoulder.

"Oh, really? I don't even want to know the specifics."

She laughed. Brock liked the sound.

Her hair, hanging just past her shoulders in three intriguing shades of brown, all intertwined to create its own enticing rainbow, slipped back, revealing a long slender neck. Brock's entire body heated. Even living a solitary life he still made time to enjoy a woman on occasion and this was definitely a woman he could enjoy.

With that thought his brow furrowed and his hands slipped into his pockets. The last thing he should be thinking about was enjoying the woman he was supposed to work with. He cleared his throat. "We should get going."

"Lead the way," she said in a voice that was way too chipper for the way he was beginning to feel.

"Wow, it's almost as warm here as it was back in Vegas," Noelle said the moment they stepped outside of the small airport.

Brock walked a step or two in front of her, not intending to be rude, rather trying to keep his mind on business where it should be. Although not blood related, Brock was just as intense and notorious when it came to a good-looking woman as the rest of the Donovan men.

The sound of her voice growing louder clued him in to how ill mannered he must appear, and so he slowed down until she caught up. A breeze, warm and thick, sifted through the air. The scent of her perfume went right up into his nose and he sighed.

"My truck's just over here," he said, directing her toward the parking lot.

As she walked beside him he noticed how tall she was. At six feet two inches, the top of most female heads came midchest to Brock. Noelle, however, was at shoulder level, which was actually the perfect kissing height. The minute that thought crossed his mind, Brock knew he was doomed.

"It was ninety-three degrees when I left Vegas, with eighty-five percent humidity," she was saying when Brock had to blink quickly and refocus once more.

Lifting a hand she pulled her hair together, then fanned the back of her neck. "What's it here, about one hundred percent humidity? I thought that since you were close to the Chesapeake Bay, it would be much cooler."

Brock took a deep breath, inhaling the sultry air of which she spoke. He needed to get a grip. She just stepped off the plane and was being nothing but cordial to him and here he was with the beginnings of sexual thoughts about a woman he'd known less than ten minutes.

"The evenings are cooler," he added, quickly cringing inwardly because he felt his remark sounded idiotic. "Here we are." Grateful, he unlocked the doors to his Ford F-350 truck and stood at the passenger side ready to help her up.

"Great ride," she commented, and there was that smile again.

Brock felt it, as plainly as she felt the heat, that little tug in his gut as her mouth spread wide, her high cheekbones made even higher. And her eyes—he'd heard it said before that eyes sparkled, he'd even seen it written in the poetry he'd been forced to read in his literature class in college. Yet Brock had always found the euphemism sappy and unrealistic, until today. Until Noelle.

Damn, he's uptight, Noelle thought the minute he slammed the door.

Pulling her seat belt over her chest and making it click, she shook her head. He was also fine as hell. Normally the rugged look wasn't her preference, but then she'd never seen a man wear a pair of jeans the way Brock Remington did. He walked with a slow precision that put you in mind of hot summer days, winding porches with white wicker furniture and tall glasses of lemonade. With his tight ass and a slow eastern drawl she'd bet there were women lined up to date him.

Okay, calm down, that's the absolute last thing she should be thinking.

Once inside he immediately started the truck and

Noelle looked out the window, giving up on casual conversation. She'd broached the usual subject, the weather, and he'd just about brushed it off, opting for more clipped answers than actual participation. So if he wanted to be quiet, she could oblige. She had a lot of things going on in her life that could bear thinking over.

Not that she was a fan of giving her problems a lot of thought. Then again, the way she'd been dealing with things so far hadn't proved successful, so why not go for the change now?

Surprise, surprise, what should be the first issue to come to mind? Luther Simmons. Now that was a chapter Noelle was glad she'd finally closed the book on. As hot and intense as their affair had been, its demise followed a similar suit. Luther had come into her life like a whirlwind. She'd met him one night at the casino, watched him lose a few grand at the blackjack table without breaking a sweat, then stopped by to speak to some of the regulars and ended up leaving the table with him. He'd waited for her to finish with her shift, at which time they'd shared her favorite cappuccino and chocolate chip cookies that evening at the restaurant.

She'd been instantly overwhelmed by his charm and his quick wit. Surely a man like this couldn't be a free agent, Noelle distinctly remembered thinking. And yet the next evening when Luther showed up at the blackjack table once more she'd been elated to see him. The physical aspect of their relationship happened fast, too fast, and before she knew it she was spending all of her free time in Luther's arms.

Finally, as were so many things in her life, her time with Luther became too good to be true. And before the end of the second month that they'd been together she found out he was married.

Leaving him alone had been a no-brainer at that point; unfortunately, Luther was the hard-headed type. For the next four weeks he'd bombarded her with phone calls and gifts and then the pop-ups at her job started. Afraid that Linc, or worse, Trent Donovan, the ex-Navy SEAL turned private investigator with a fuse as short as her baby finger, would find out, and on the advice of her friend, Karena, she'd obtained a restraining order. Somebody probably should have warned her that those pieces of paper were just about worthless when it came to a man like Luther.

He wasn't your typical stalker in that he wasn't slashing her tires or breaking into her house—which would have been almost suicidal, since she still lived with Jade and Linc. No, instead, Luther sent her text messages, e-mails and letters by mail, all asking her to give him another chance, to give their love another chance. Luther was definitely not a threat—he was what they called a lover, not a fighter. So in the twisted world of stalkers, Luther was very low on the totem pole and Noelle was not afraid of him.

What she was, however, was tired. Sick and tired, to be correct, of all the drama. It seemed as if her entire life had revolved around the word. Whether she was a magnet for it or somehow thrived from the chaos, it was always there.

She'd told Jade a little bit about Luther, only because her sister was a constant worrywart where she was concerned and when she overheard a heated conversation Noelle was having on the phone with Luther, she'd questioned her. Jade had wanted to run directly to Linc, but Noelle had stopped her. Thank God.

The last thing she wanted was to bring this type of mess into the Donovan family. They'd all been so nice and loving to her over these past two years that she owed them so much more than to have some crazy married man trying to win back the affection she'd so foolishly given him.

"Cheer up. My house is air-conditioned," Brock said as he watched her still sitting in the seat staring straight ahead. He'd gotten out of the car and had been holding the door open for a few minutes now, waiting for her to get out.

When she still hadn't moved he touched a hand to her arm. She jerked, then those hypnotic eyes found his. He swallowed and willed himself not to have any other reaction. "You all right?"

"Yes," she said, her voice just a little agitated because for a moment she'd forgotten where she was and who she was with. "I'm fine." Pulling her arm out of his reach, she jumped down from the cab.

And just like that she moved past him, walking along the pathway toward the side door of his house. Taking her luggage out of the car, Brock figured that whatever was on her mind was her business. The fact that she now looked almost haunted shouldn't have bothered him. And yet, it did.

His house was gorgeous. As far as spacious rooms, hardwood floors and a terrific view of the water went. However, it was a little on the empty side where furniture was concerned.

The concept that less meant…well, less, continued

on into the kitchen where alongside the stainless steel appliances and on top of the blue-flecked granite countertop was a coffeemaker, with the smallest coffeepot Noelle had ever seen. Next to the pot was a medium-sized canister of decaffeinated coffee in a pretty average brand. There was a dishwasher but it looked barely used, no fingerprints at or near the handle as you'd usually see with stainless steel. Beside the dish drainer to the right of the double sink she spied a mug, one bowl and one spoon inside it, probably left over from his breakfast. It was quite neat for the kitchen of a man, riding close to the definition of sterile. However, it fit right along with Brock's seemingly uptight demeanor.

But it was when they walked out onto the screened porch with its brick-encased fireplace that Noelle felt something slightly different. The furniture was made of heavy oak with deep, inviting cushions in a soft caramel tone. Rugs, not Oriental but plush and functional, aligned the tiled floor. There were coffee tables and end tables, but they only held lamps and the remote control to the entertainment system that lined one entire wall, she assumed. The fireplace looked well used, just as the chair closest to it. He sat there, she imagined, put his feet up on the table and read one of the books stuffed into the bookshelf in the living room.

"You spend a lot of time out here?" she asked, letting her hand touch the softness of the chair before sitting down.

"I do," he admitted with a slightly questioning tone.

"You're not a man of many words, are you?" Noelle asked, already assuming she'd get another one- to two-word response.

"I get by."

She nodded and retained a knowing grin. This was going to be a long, dismal summer for her—getting by on his sparse answers and trying to make sense of them.

"So let's talk about the casino," she said because there was no use trying to discuss anything else. Brock Remington was not a talker. That was fine—she wasn't here to talk or to get to know him. She was here to work and that's all she planned to do, no matter how well he wore his jeans.

Chapter 3

It was all about business, Brock reminded himself as he pulled out the blueprints he'd retrieved from his office and laid them on the coffee table on the porch in front of her. She bent forward, letting her elbows rest on her knees as she surveyed them.

She wore jeans, fitted to perfection, he might add, and a T-shirt with "Las Vegas" in glittering, swirling letters across her breasts. If Brock had ever wanted to be something in his next life it would be those letters. Looking as if it was costing her dearly to sit still, she tapped her feet on the floor while she studied the papers.

For a moment Brock wondered if she even knew what she was looking at, then chastised himself for assuming that just because she was gorgeous and stacked like a *Playboy* magazine model that she didn't have an ounce of sense. Linc had told him how she'd obtained her degree and still took managerial classes to keep sharp on the job. He'd be wise to remember that instead of the way that denim hugged her plump bottom.

"This is a different concept you've used," she was saying.

Taking a seat in his favorite chair, Brock nodded. "Most casinos are designed to spread out, with gaming facilities going horizontally and hotel towers on top. My architect and I decided to break from the norm. Luckily Linc approved."

She nodded. "I can see why he did."

Taking that as a compliment, Brock cracked a small smile. "Do you like it?"

He wasn't prepared for her to look up at him in response, but she did. She didn't smile, but the twinkle in her eye said she was pleased. "I do. I think it's more than functional—it's unique. Having a dash of gaming, entertainment and suites on each floor is a great opportunity for us to capitalize on every guest."

"Exactly. The idea is that no matter where the guest goes in the facility they'll have options of where and how to spend their money."

"And that's the name of the game."

She did smile then and he joined her, relaxing a bit. She was in his space, a place where he normally didn't allow women he barely knew. But since he'd known they would need to work long grueling hours to get the Gramercy II up and running, he'd been the one to suggest to Linc that she simply stay at the house with him instead of getting a hotel room. Surprisingly, both Linc and Noelle had thought that a wise idea.

When they'd toured the house he'd been on edge, wondering what she thought about what she was seeing. He didn't put a lot of time and energy into decorating, much to Josette's dismay. He functioned on the bare necessities, which could come off as sparse to some. But since he never entertained, beyond having Josette and Kent over to light up the grill, it didn't matter.

Speaking of which, he said, "I planned to put a couple of steaks on the grill for dinner. Is that okay with you?"

"Ah, yeah. That's fine. I like steak."

He nodded. "Good."

"What I don't like are all these windows."

Brock looked around and frowned. "It's a screened porch," he said in defense.

"What? Oh, no, not here. The porch is nice. It's comfortable and probably relaxing after a long day's work." She tapped a finger to the blueprint. "I'm talking about at the casino. You have to know that reminding the guest of the time distracts them from gambling. They'll realize how long they've been at one table if they can see that when they came in it was daylight and now it's dark."

He felt like an idiot. Of course she was talking about the casino.

"Normally that's true," he said, clearing his throat. "But we've designed some special effects lighting that will change the moods. So the guest isn't reminded of the time but entranced by the ambiance."

She looked to be thinking that over, her hair brushing over her shoulders as she nodded. "That might work. Now what about here? What's this?"

"The waterfall cove," he answered. "People in this

region are in love with the water so we decided to keep that as the recurring theme. Instead of something as ostentatious and played out as pyramids and Egyptian or Venetian themes, we thought we'd simply let nature take its course, per se."

"Your architect is a genius. Who's the interior designer? I'll need to meet with them sometime this week to go over how this theme is being incorporated. I think something subtle, classic lines, use of basic materials, copper, bronze, stuff like that will go well with the natural flow. Oh, and I want to make sure we're being as green as possible."

"Green?"

"Yes, as in the environment. Wherever possible we need to conserve, recycle, save the Earth."

Brock held up a hand as she looked like she would go into more explanation. "I get it. Kent Foster is the architect. He has an even more talented wife. Come to think of it, she's better looking than Kent, too." He laughed. "I've contracted her for the interior designing."

"Keeping it all in the family, huh?"

Brock instantly sobered. "They're not my family," he snapped, and the air around them chilled.

It was like walking on eggshells, Noelle thought dismally. She'd replayed their conversation in her mind at least three times since he'd bolted up out of the chair and began readying the grill for their steak dinner, she supposed.

After the third time she figured to hell with it. If he was some crazy, emotional head case she could do without that drama. Hadn't she had enough of that going on in her life already? No, she definitely was not in the mood. Therefore, her next thought was that she had no intention of dealing with Brock Remington on any level other than their work on the casino. In that area he seemed knowledgeable, confident, not nearly as agitated.

From the moment she'd introduced herself to him he'd acted as if she'd done something to offend him personally. Which, by the way, in her past could have been entirely true. But Noelle was no longer that immature girl. She'd grown in the years she'd known the Donovans, in the time she'd watched her sister find the happiness she deserved. So again, she had no idea what Brock's problem was.

Hearing her cell phone chime, she stood, walked to where she'd placed her purse on the chair closest to the doorway that led into the house and retrieved it. After checking her caller ID first, she breathed a sigh of relief to see it was Jade.

"Hi," Noelle said with a smile.

"Hi. You didn't call when you landed so I worried."

"You always worry."

"That's what big sisters do. So how's it going? How was the plane ride? Is the Eastern Shore as beautiful in the summer as the brochure says? How's Brock? Are you being nice to him?"

"Whoa, hold on with the interrogation." Noelle chuckled then looked over her shoulder to see that Brock still had his back to her, still focusing on getting the grill started. But as a precaution Noelle moved into the foyer of the house, out of his earshot.

"The plane ride wasn't as bad as I thought. Flying on

a private jet is much more relaxing than going commercial. As for the scenery, from what I've seen it's nice. Lots of trees and grass and pretty flowers. It's hot as hell here, though."

"You're used to the heat."

"No, Vegas heat is dry. This is sticky, sultry, but I shall survive."

"Ok, so how's Brock? Linc said he just had his house built a couple of years ago. Is it nice?"

"It's a beautiful home. And it's right on the water. There's a small village just a few miles away that he said we'd visit maybe tomorrow to get more of the Eastern Shore feel. But I had a tour of the house and it's okay, if you like this sort of thing."

"What's that supposed to mean?"

Even though she knew Jade couldn't see her, Noelle shrugged. "I mean, it's really nice, a little sparse for my tastes, but I get the impression he's a man with minimal needs."

"Where is he now?"

"Making dinner."

"Oh, a man that cooks. That's heavenly. Linc can barely warm a bottle for the girls, let alone cook a meal."

"Calm down—it's on the grill. That's like second nature to them. If a man can't handle a grill, he's got real issues."

Jade laughed. "Well, I just wanted to check up on you and make sure things were going smoothly."

I wouldn't exactly say smoothly, she thought, remembering the way Brock had just about raced away from her and their conversation. "I'm not on vacation, Jade. We're going over the plans for the casino and I suspect we'll get right to work tomorrow. It's no big deal."

"It's just that you've never been this far away from me, so allow me a little worry for the time being."

"I'm fine." While Jade loved the progress Noelle had made—loved the fact that Noelle was no longer partying all night, sleeping most of the day, and basically tossing her life away—she still felt the need to protect her. Noelle respected that to a certain extent because for so long she had depended on her sister for everything—but now she didn't, now she was standing on her own two feet. No matter what sticky situations they still seemed to walk her into.

"You have two beautiful daughters to worry about now. I'm a big girl. If I can't get myself out of the trouble I get into, then that's my problem."

"Are you in trouble? What really happened with Luther, Noelle? Because you never did tell me a lot about him or why you two stopped seeing each other. All I know is that he had some issues letting go."

"No," she answered quickly. "Luther is definitely not a situation. Besides, that's over and done with and I'm not looking for another relationship until I can find a man who likes me for me and not just my physical attributes."

Jade sighed. "Listen to you. I remember a time when your physical attributes were your best asset. That's what you used to say."

"Yeah, well, that ship has sailed," Noelle responded. "There's a new sheriff in town and she's taking no prisoners so any man that steps to me now better be for real about being with me or else he can just keep on steppin'."

"I hear you, little sis. And you're right. You deserve more than a man that simply wants you in his bed."

"And that's what I plan to get." Noelle sighed. "Even if I have to grow old and gray waiting for it."

Jade chuckled. "Me, I can see growing old and gray. You, on the other hand, will be fifty years old and counting with your hair dyed blond, your party dress on and, oh yes, the hottest, most expensive designer shoes you can find."

Noelle couldn't help but smile—her sister knew her all too well.

Chapter 4

"I apologize for earlier," Brock said after they'd finished cleaning up their dinner dishes. Although after Noelle's phone call she'd come back out onto the porch as if nothing had happened between them, he felt horrible for the way he'd handled her innocent comment.

It wasn't her fault he had no real family. And truth be told, the Donovans had been more than welcoming to him. But Brock longed for a blood tie, a real live connection to the people he'd been born from. That's why he'd come back to Maryland, to be closer to them, hoping that maybe, just maybe, his mother would come around.

Unfortunately, that wasn't meant to be.

He'd long since stopped going to see his mother at the psychiatric hospital. She had no idea who he was anyway. A search for any other relatives had proved unsuccessful. So it was just him in this world, the last surviving Remington. That thought made him sad more often than Brock liked to admit.

But that gave him no right to take it out on Noelle. Especially since over dinner he'd finally realized what his real issue with her was. He was attracted to her.

That seemed simple enough. Boy meets girl, boy likes what he sees, boy wants girl. Discreet glances to her left hand showed no rings and no shadow of a ring, so he figured she was free. Yet why a man hadn't laid his claim to her yet was beyond Brock. If he were the type, he certainly would have. It was a good thing he had no intentions of claiming any woman, ever.

Shrugging, she was already heading for the steps. "Already forgotten," she said brightly. "I'm just going to head on up to bed. Plane rides aren't my favorite so I didn't get a lot of rest last night from worrying about it. I know it should probably feel earlier to me, still, I'm tired. What time are we heading to the casino in the morning?"

Brock was right behind her, after switching off the only lights they'd used on the downstairs level. He'd locked the house up while she cleaned the countertops in the kitchen. Watching her bottom as she leaned over the granite top had become more than a little uncomfortable so he'd opted for some space. Now, however, with her standing on the step above him, he was afforded yet another gracious view of her gorgeous body.

It should be a sin, he told himself when he'd seen her for the first time at the airport. A sin and a shame that God created such a beautifully enticing woman. Keeping his hands off her was not a viable option, Brock finally decided.

"I thought we could tour St. Michaels, then head back up the coast toward Easton and the construction site. I've asked Kent and Josette to meet us there around noon."

"That sounds good," she said, and began walking up the stairs.

Brock followed with his eyes glued to the alluring sway of her hips, the generous curve of her bottom. She had long legs with meaty thighs. Brock was definitely into women who had some meat on their bones. Although thin might be in for some, he preferred having something solid to hold on to in bed.

Noelle Vincent was definitely solid. With her height she was evenly proportioned, with curves and thickness that had his mouth watering. It had been quite some time since he'd had such a strong physical reaction to a woman. According to Kent, way too long. He'd have to thank Linc for sending him this surprise package.

The mere thought of Linc and this project brought forth questions of whether or not it was wise to cross the line with Noelle. A couple of hours ago he'd been worried about her holding up the project, but not in this way. As with everything else in his life, Brock liked to play his cards close to the vest. So he vowed that the inevitable seduction of the enticing Noelle Vincent would be slow, drawn out and extremely pleasing.

With that out of the way the question still remained: How would making a move on Noelle play against their casino business? Generally speaking, people who were working together didn't do well in relationships. But because Brock clearly wasn't looking for a relationship, she was fair game.

That's where his thoughts were leaning when she stopped in front of the door to the guest room he'd told her was hers. He'd left her bags in there earlier but hadn't been paying much attention to walking so when she stopped he bumped into her.

"Slow down," she said, turning and placing both her palms on his chest to stop him.

As their bodies touched, something inside Brock clicked as if falling right into place. "Sorry about that," he said immediately but couldn't make himself take a step backward, a step away from her.

"I'd say you were intoxicated but I know you only had an iced tea with dinner. Which was very tasty, by the way. Jade was impressed by a man that could cook. I'll have to tell her that you did the job very well."

He chuckled, and Noelle felt little twinges in her stomach. He hadn't laughed once during dinner. It was a nice sound, deep and rich. His eyes crinkled ever so slightly at the corners when he did and she figured he obviously didn't laugh often. *Pity,* she thought.

Brock Remington was a very nice-looking man, with his bronzed skin and close-cut dark brown hair. The strong bone structure of his face could be presumed as intimidating, but Noelle thought it showed strength and endurance. His eyes were a light shade of brown, not as light as hers but certainly not as dark as his hair. He had a great body—she'd already checked that out when they were downstairs—and his attire was casual yet attractive. Jeans and Timberland boots had never looked so good on a man to her before. His

Ralph Lauren polo shirt was a summery shade of coral, which was a great accent to his complexion. In short, he was quite a tasty morsel to look at. If one were looking, that is.

"You talked to your sister about me already?"

He was more than in her space, backing her up against the door. Surely this was inappropriate…but that didn't stop it from feeling good.

"She called earlier and asked how things were going. I told her you were being very hospitable."

"Even though at that point I wasn't?"

Noelle waved a hand. "I told you that was already forgotten. I may have been a little out of line. Sometimes my mouth moves faster than my brain. It's a horrible habit that's gotten me into lots of trouble."

He cocked his head to the side, his eyes fixated on the mouth she spoke of. "Trouble, huh? I can just imagine."

Right there, in that hallway where they stood, the temperature seemed to rise another fifty degrees, so that tiny beads of sweat had begun to form in the valley between her breasts. That, coupled with his proximity and the timbre his voice had lowered to when he'd just spoken gave Noelle a slight start. If she didn't know better she'd think…

Before she could actually finish that thought, his hand was cupping the nape of her neck, pulling her the half step closer that landed her chest flush against his.

"It's such a pretty mouth. When I look at it I can only imagine good things," he said gruffly.

This wasn't right, some distant voice spoke in the back of her mind. This wasn't what she was here for. And yet she'd seemed to fit against his strong body so perfectly. His mouth somehow knowing exactly how to work hers. Her thighs quivered as in her mind's eye she could see them together, naked, rolling over a big bed, bodies entwined with one goal in mind—pleasure, mindless, earth-shattering pleasure.

That part moved fast, going into a blur and then there was nothing…once more, for Noelle, there was nothing left.

Her brain attempted to protest and had just sent the message to her mouth, which had opened to do its bidding, when bam!

His lips touched hers, his tongue slipping quickly inside, stroking hers until the heat that surrounded them was transferred directly into her body. From his lips to hers the fire climbed, swarming through her body until her arms were instinctively lifting, wrapping around his neck as his moved to her waist, slipping farther to cup her bottom.

And there she was, back pressed against the bedroom door, his strong hands lifting her until only the tips of her toes touched the floor. She felt trapped, absorbed and terribly aroused all at once. The dance of his tongue around hers made her dizzy, but she didn't miss a step, opening her mouth wider, tilting her head to take him deeper.

Brock groaned, his fingers digging into the soft skin of her backside. She felt so good against him this had to be a crime or an explicit-as-hell dream. She was kissing him back, this pretty woman he'd just met. Kissing him with a hunger that matched his own.

His erection pounded against his zipper, demanding release. He ground into her, lifting her off the floor, letting his hands move down to her thighs to wrap their solid length around his waist.

Her center was flush against his erection. His hips jerked instinctively. Full breasts pressed against his chest and the blood pounded fiercely in Brock's ears.

Then she made an indecipherable sound, and through the haze of desire he felt her struggling to break free of his grasp. The word *no* echoed in his mind, even though he knew she couldn't possibly have said anything because his lips were still devouring hers. Still, her palms pressing urgently against his chest and her thighs trying to squirm down from him could mean only one thing. Without the conscious consent of his body, his mind roared for him to stop. And when that message finally filtered through, Brock released her completely, taking a step back.

Noelle fell backward against the door with a thump but miraculously remained upright. She looked up at him, unable or unwilling to speak, Brock wasn't quite sure. Then she was gone, disappearing behind the door in seconds.

As the door to her room clicked shut Brock inhaled a deep, steadying breath.

So much for seducing her slowly.

Chapter 5

So they kissed, that wasn't so bad. Over and over Noelle told herself this as she moved silently through Brock's house, passing the porch where they'd shared a nice platonic steak dinner last night. That had been only an hour before he'd kissed her and she'd acted like a deprived sex fiend, crawling all over him as if she just couldn't get enough.

It wasn't quite six yet, but the sky was already brightening, the morning coming whether she wanted to face it or not. Now, was it through this door and around to the left or around to the right? Brock had shown her the pool during the tour yesterday. One thing she'd become accustomed to living in Jade and Linc's spacious home was the indoor and outdoor pools. So the majority of her mornings either started with a brisk run or a couple of laps. Because she didn't know this area well, Noelle had opted for a swim. She was meeting with Brock in a few hours, so thinking about the kiss and its effect on her would have to wait. Or she'd simply bypass it altogether.

That was one of her other talents—one that she hadn't figured out whether was good or bad. She could push things aside, put them in their own compartment and pull them out and deal with them when she was ready. And right now, she thought as just a few short feet away—after making the left turn—she'd spotted the pool, she wasn't ready to deal with the attraction to Brock Remington.

Moving quickly, Noelle dropped her towel on one of the lounge chairs and headed straight for the water. She could dip a toe in to test the water but where was the fun in that? Instead, she dove right in, going almost to the bottom then paddling herself up to the top. Breaking through the water she spewed a bit and took a deep breath. Pushing her wet hair out of her eyes she lay back into a seamless backstroke.

When the sun finally made its appearance, Noelle felt its warm persistent rays against her skin as she continued to move throughout the water.

It was really pretty here, quaint and scenic. So much so that she probably would have never thought to put a new casino in this area. This was either a place for lovers or retirees, like one of those complexes in Florida—Lake Buena something or other.

But Linc had done his research and she'd read the reports. Just forty-five minutes to the south there was a slots-only casino and north in Delaware there was another slots-only casino, with another one in West Virginia. Maryland was prime for a full-fledged gaming facility. The state already boasted a world-class race course at Pimlico, but the Gramercy II would offer gaming beyond horse racing. It was a gold mine and Linc was determined to tap into it.

Coming out of the pool for the first time, Noelle ran to the chair where she'd dropped her towel and dried off her face. Holding her head to one side, she waited for the water to drain out. She hated that echoing when water was stuck in her ears, but she hated wearing earplugs even more. So after checking her watch and confirming she had more time, she headed for the pool once more. Just a few more laps, then she'd head into the house to get ready to meet Brock.

His name resonated in her mind as she moved sleekly through the water. She allowed her thoughts to circle around him for a moment. Attractive in a rugged, outdoorsy kind of way was what he was. Not the polished money men she dealt with back in Vegas, that was for sure. He was kind of quiet, uptight and definitely on edge about something. Still, his body was the bomb, muscles rippling from every part of him. She'd bet it came more from working right alongside his construction crew than from working out inside any upscale gym.

And, as far as she was concerned he delivered one whopper of a kiss. Her body still tingled when she thought about their exchange. But it was just that, a kiss, nothing more. Which should probably be the story of her life with men. The physical was always easy. It always came first, hot and fast. Then like a one-alarm fire being attacked by a hose, it smoldered, leaving in its wake the charred remains of what could have been.

Well, Noelle Vincent was tired of getting burned.

She swam more quickly now, trying to outrun her

past, the mistakes, the pain. Her lungs were just beginning to burn for air when she felt something snake around her waist. On impulse she squirmed, turning to see what had grabbed her. But it was too late—the grip was tight and she was headed for the top without even having to tread water herself.

Sucking in air she opened her eyes, then flung around quickly, ready to punch, scratch and scream her way free, only to find herself face-to-face with the man she had a sinking feeling was up to no good.

"Mornin'," he said, his smile not really matching the heated gleam in his eyes.

"Good morning," she managed, wiping her hair out of her face.

Brock lifted a hand, moved another strand away from her eyes. "Heard you down here and decided a swim looked like a good idea."

He had thick eyebrows. She hadn't noticed that last night, but she did now because he was really close to her and she was attempting to keep her gaze above the shoulders because it was clear he wore no shirt.

"I was just finishing up," she said. "I need to go and get dressed."

He caught her arm when she attempted to swim away. "No. Stay." Pulling her close again, this time he cupped her chin. "Please."

In the most nonchalant voice she could conjure, Noelle said, "Sure. Why not?"

Brock released a breath with her words. For a moment he thought she was going to be all awkward and bothered by their kiss. The kiss that had kept him up most of the night. But she seemed to be pretty relaxed as she swam slowly beside him. They watched each other between strokes but didn't speak. She looked confident, self-assured as she cut through the water. He liked that. It convinced him that his instincts about her had been right. She wasn't one of those starry-eyed women who took a kiss to mean the beginning of some life-changing relationship.

That wasn't what Brock needed in his life. He'd had enough emotional issues without adding more. Besides, he had nothing to offer a woman on a long-term basis, nothing at all.

But right now, at this very moment he knew what he wanted to offer Noelle Vincent. He wanted her—there was absolutely no doubt about that. Beneath him, on top of him—each and every possible position had run quickly through his mind.

When he'd heard the water and looked out his window to see her in the pool this morning, his desire to be close to her had only heightened. She wore a bikini that showed more than it hid. His mouth had literally begun to water, his erection growing so hard it had taken several minutes and thoughts of the last few World Series baseball games to get it to go down enough for him to comfortably slip into his swim trunks.

So deep in his lavacious thoughts of her it took a moment before Brock realized she'd stopped swimming.

"What? Is something wrong?" he asked, treading water as he looked back at her.

"No. This is just so boring. Since we're both out here I was thinking…".

What were you thinking? Brock found himself with

a ridiculous urge to hear all her thoughts, to know any and everything about her. She was even prettier first thing in the morning with her hair soaking wet, no makeup and a bathing suit that would send a blind geriatric man into cardiac arrest.

"Let's race!" she suggested with an exuberant smile.

Now that was the very last thing Brock had imagined or hoped she'd say.

"Race? I don't think so," he began.

"Oh, come on, don't be such a dud."

Smacking her hands against the water, she smiled as it splashed in his face. Brock blinked the droplets away, not sure if he'd just been insulted or not.

"Unless you're afraid to be beaten by a girl." She batted her long lashes and gave a sweeter than natural smile.

Brock caught the competitive gleam in her eye. She was certainly a surprise. Bright and chipper so early in the morning and manipulative, too. Oh yeah, he was liking her more and more by the second. She'd suggested the race, but Brock was going to make sure the results turned out in his favor.

"What do I get if I win?" he asked.

"Hmm," she thought for a minute. "My admiration for loosening up enough to race in the first place."

"Okay," Brock said slowly. He could accept her admiring him. But he wanted more. "And what else?"

"A 'congratulations,'" she answered with a raised brow.

"Add a congratulatory hug *and* kiss and I'm game."

Noelle contemplated a moment. Kissing Brock again would be dangerous, she knew, and potentially fatal to her newfound resolve. But there were no worries—he wouldn't win.

"Deal." She reached out a hand only to be startled by the instant warmth when his connected with hers in what should have been a friendly shake. It was weird and made her uncomfortable so she pulled away.

Brock's smile never wavered. "Need a handicap, pretty lady?"

Her answer was another splash of water in his face. "Only if you do."

Laughter bubbled in his chest as he smiled. "Four lengths," he said as they made their way to the end of the pool.

"On your mark," she said keeping her eye on the other side of the pool.

"Go!" he yelled and they both pushed off.

Brock was a swimmer, she probably should have guessed that by the size of his pool, but still she'd challenged him. And as far as he could see, she was going neck and neck with him.

Slapping the wall they headed off for the second length. She was beautiful, more so than just the nice body and pretty smile. She cut through the water with a sleek grace that rivaled any Olympic swimmer. Never backing down, never slowing, she kept up with him without even panting. He was beyond impressed.

On the third length Brock picked up, waiting to catch the win, but she kept up with him, just a head behind. He was still holding back, toying with the idea of letting her win, since she was a guest in his house and all that. Then he thought of her feisty personality, her teasing little dare, the way she'd kissed him so passionately last night without hesitation, without regret. Noelle Vincent was not a woman to be discounted in any way, shape or form, least of all a swim race that she'd initiated.

So Brock let loose, passing her by a full body length as he reached his long arm out and tapped the wall almost thirty seconds before her.

Noelle came up behind him, heart hammering in her chest. She'd known the exact moment he'd stopped playing with her and appreciated him all the more for it. If she were going to lose, it had better be to someone who was strong enough to race at their full potential and not give her some egotistical female handicap.

The race had been exhilarating and she was pumped. So much so that the ramifications of his winner's reward fled from her mind the moment he came closer, snaking his arm around her waist and pulling her up against his chest.

"Now the winner takes the prize," he said, lowering his head until their lips were a breath away.

It felt so right—his tight grip around her waist, the close proximity of their bodies—that she could see no problems, no issues to hold her back. His gaze held hers and she quite simply melted against him. If this were the prize, she might be tempted to lose to him more often.

Chapter 6

Kiss number two was even more spine tingling than the first, and when Brock's fingers slid beneath the rim of her bikini bottom Noelle was ready to beg.

Hungrily his mouth ravaged hers as they stood in the shallow end of the pool. Again her arms slipped effortlessly around his neck. Why this man she barely knew had this effect on her was a fleeting thought in her mind.

His fingers stroked her center, with the same heated sensations as his tongue.

She shivered and he groaned.

"I want you," he said simply, his lips gliding along the line of her jaw.

Noelle had a moment or two to contemplate the words before he was kissing her again. Scraping her toes against the bottom of the pool, she knew this wasn't a dream. But how was it that just yesterday morning she was waking in her own bed, swimming in the pool she'd become accustomed to in the last two years and now she was here, in Maryland, kissing this man, loving the feel of his muscled body against hers? This was fast. *Too fast,* her rational brain said.

But, oh, so good, was the unanimous decision as one word slipped from her lips. "Yes."

Her legs were wrapped securely around his waist while he supported her with one hand to her neck. The other hand had slipped quickly between their bodies, pushing aside her swimsuit bottom, searching and finding.

Noelle gasped, letting her head fall back as the sensations rippled through her with the ferocity of a summer storm.

"You're so ready for me," Brock groaned in her ear. "Were you thinking of this all night like I was?"

She couldn't speak, didn't dare utter a word for fear of it coming out in a voice she didn't recognize. Her response was only a jerk of her hips as one finger slipped into her tight passage.

His shoulders were slippery as she tried to hold on, her nails scraping along his light skin. There would probably be marks there later but right now she couldn't be concerned with that.

"Tell me what you want," he pressed her as his tongue traced a heated path from her ear down to her neck.

"Dammit!" Noelle cursed. The emotions swirling through her were almost too much to bear, the controversy flying like fierce lightning bolts.

Brock had no idea her cursing was due to the war going on between her mind and her body when he said, "Tell me what you need and I'll give it to you."

Her mind was quickly losing the battle.

She shouldn't be doing this, not with him, not now. But she couldn't stop him, didn't really want to stop him. Each thrust of his finger pressed deeper inside of her, rubbing against sensitive muscles, pushing her closer to a blissful release.

"Tell me and I'll give it to you."

She hadn't said it, but Brock felt it. They both wanted the same thing. Her heart pounded as frantically as his own, their need too urgent, too feral to be denied. So pulling his hand from her enticing warmth he freed his aching erection and followed the trail to ecstasy.

The moment he was inside her they both stilled. Above, the sun rose higher in the sky, its intense rays beaming down on them. Around them the chlorine-tinted water rippled, giving their bodies a buoyed sensation that only seemed to stroke their desire.

"Yes," she moaned.

"Hell, yes!" Brock roared, pulled out slightly, then slamming back into her heated center.

In fevered motions they both pumped and groaned until the end was all they could see, the glorious release all they could comprehend.

Her thighs tightened around his waist, her nails beginning to break the skin on his shoulders. Her entire body shivered and she let loose one slow, long moan that vibrated in the air.

On that note Brock pulled out halfway, holding his body stiffly as he slid back into her for a second and third time. Then everything went hazy as his release slammed into him like a tidal wave. He held her close, hoping he didn't crush her but defenseless against the urge.

For endless moments they just stood there, trying to catch their breath. Brock shifted first as Noelle's head was resting on his shoulder, her face hidden from him. Without a word, he scooped her up by the knees and carried her to the edge of the pool where the steps were. Climbing out, he left the towels and headed straight for the house, straight for his bedroom, where he should have taken her in the first place if he'd been thinking logically.

The bedroom seemed to be a million miles away as Brock finally carried Noelle through the door.

Setting her gently onto his bed Brock watched her wrap her arms around herself and shiver. He retrieved a towel from the bathroom and wrapped it around her shoulders.

She took a deep breath and looked up at him then. Her light eyes lacked that spark he'd first noticed in them yesterday. Instead they seemed tinged with something akin to sadness. Immediately Brock felt like an ass.

Not only had they just met yesterday, but he'd taken her fast and hot in a pool as if they were teenagers. As a result this felt like an awkward morning after. The problem was, Brock didn't do morning afters. Sex at the female's house was his choice. It afforded him the perfect escape plan—he could get up and leave whenever he got ready, which was always before morning. But Noelle was here, in his house, in his bed. They were working together on an important project and would be spending a great deal of time together for the next three months.

Leaving her at the pool wasn't going to work, not that he'd even considered doing anything that childish and disgraceful.

"I apologize," he started. "I didn't plan for this to happen. Not out there in the pool and—"

She held up a hand to stop his words.

"Saying we got carried away is an understatement," she said quietly.

No, Brock thought. There was no escaping the tremendous amount of guilt he felt. Strands of dark wet hair lay flat against her head, some sticking to her face. Lifting a hand gently he pushed them back, then paused at her elegantly arched eyebrow and eyes that pinned him with a serious gaze.

"Yeah, that's an understatement, all right," he said. The funny thing about his escape plan was that, at this very moment, even if it were possible, Brock was certain he wouldn't have acted on it.

Noelle sat up straighter and squared her shoulders. "Good, we agree on that point. This project we're working on is important to Linc and so it's important to me. I won't let him down."

"I didn't think you would."

"Okay." She nodded. "We're clear on another point. So there's no need to tell him about our momentary lapse in judgment."

Her words seemed cold and distant, which really shouldn't have bothered him. Still, Brock wasn't entirely sure that he liked them. "Is that what this was?"

"Yes. Of course it was. Neither of us were thinking straight. It was early and we had that vigorous swim. We're the only two people in this house, for Pete's sake! A physical attraction would be imminent. So we acted on it and it's done. We've gotten it out of our system and it's now time to move on."

She was talking so fast and she was still in that barely there swimsuit, although the towel tried to cover most of her exposed skin. He was kneeling in front of her, thankfully, so the fact that he was becoming aroused again was currently his secret. Still, Brock found it difficult to keep up. "Okay," he finally managed.

Then she was moving, getting up off the bed. "I'm glad we see eye to eye on this. I'll be ready for our meeting in an hour," she said, reaching for the doorknob, then pausing.

Never turning back to him she said in a voice that was quiet and just on the side of sad, "This is not who I am. I don't do this anymore." With that she slipped out the door.

Brock was left with nothing to do or say but stare at the spot where she'd been. In the span of an hour he'd awakened, gone for a swim, shared in the most explosive sex of his life with a pretty woman and was now alone again in his bedroom. Was it all a dream?

Hell no! Each touch, each kiss, each moan was as real as his now-withering arousal. And sadly enough, so was her quick and efficient, yet troubled and piercing, departure.

Standing up, he then fell on the bed and sighed. "Good morning to me."

Noelle slouched against the door to her room, which she'd just closed tightly. Her head lolled back and she shut her eyes. How could she have been so stupid?

"Dammit! Dammit! Dammit!" she hissed, punctuating each word with a fist to her thigh.

Hadn't she convinced herself that she was going to

change? She was going to be different with future relationships. Hadn't she learned anything from dealing
with Luther? Obviously not.

Forcing herself to move away from the door, Noelle
went to the closet where she'd hung most of her clothes
yesterday. Retrieving a linen pantsuit that should stand
up against the sweltering heat and allow her to appear
professional at the same time, she moved to the bed and
dropped her clothes there. Then she looked down at
herself. She'd had sex with her boss's cousin, in his
pool, after knowing him for less than twenty-four hours.
The boss's cousin who she would be working closely
with for the next few months. Could her life possibly
get any worse than this?

Yes, it definitely could, she thought with horror. *They
hadn't even used a condom!*

Growling like a caged animal, Noelle grabbed clean
underwear and made her way into the bathroom, immediately switching the shower on to hot water. Standing
in the mirror she went ahead and chucked the bikini,
then simply looked at herself. Who was this person and
why was she so prone to make the same mistakes over
and over again? Slapping her palms down onto the
vanity, she allowed a few moments to break down. No,
she didn't cry because tears were like foreign objects to
her after Grammy's passing.

It had been almost four years now since the grandmother who had raised Noelle and Jade had died, but
the pain sometimes was still fresh. If she were here,
Noelle knew without a doubt that Grammy would not
be pleased. She was less than pleased herself. After the
affair with Luther she'd sworn that being intimate with

a man before she really got to know him was a mistake, one that she'd never make again. And yet, here she was in that same predicament not even a year later.

But it wasn't too late. It was never too late to change. This was a lesson Noelle had already learned. So immediately regrouping she stepped into the shower. This was just a temporary setback—she still had a job to do. Still had yet another point to prove to Linc and then to herself. She was attracted to Brock Remington—that much was clear. He was attracted to her but he wasn't what she needed right now, he couldn't be. How she knew this for certain, Noelle didn't even have the time to contemplate. She needed to get dressed and to go on with business as planned. Just as she told Brock, they would put this digression behind them and they would move forward. She could do this, she knew she could, she told herself as she lifted her face to the spray of warm water.

She was not the same immature, out-of-control woman she'd been while Grammy was alive. She was different. Her life was different and she intended to prove that point to everyone she knew.

Her own vanilla-scented soap that she'd brought with her was in the soap dish and she scooped it up, lathering it over her body, all the while chanting *I can do this. I will do this.*

That diatribe had carried her through the grooming process, but it was when she'd stood dressed and made up, ready to leave, that she faltered. The bravado she liked to display was slipping just a little. Standing at the bedroom door, one hand on the knob, the other holding her purse, Noelle once again grappled for control.

She wasn't a bad person, she knew this. Bad things

just happened to her all the time. Still what had transpired between her and Brock wasn't too bad. Or was it? She was on the brink of screaming—she hated the conflicting thoughts that filled her mind to the point of making her dizzy—when her cell phone rang.

Thankful for the interruption, she stepped back from the door and retrieved the phone from her purse.

"Hey, girl! How does it feel to finally be on the east coast?"

The cheerful, high-pitched voice belonged to Noelle's closest friend who was not related by blood or marriage, Karena Lakefield. They'd met when Karena was giving a lecture at the college on buying art through different media and interpreting quotes. As the buyer and director of sales for the reputed Lakefield Museum of New York Karena was top in her field. Noelle had been taking an art class and attended the lecture to broaden her horizons in that area because at the time Linc had wanted all the rooms of the Gramercy I spruced up with African-American art.

After the class Noelle still had a few questions and Karena suggested they have lunch. From that point on they'd been instant friends, the cell phone being another of their closest companions since Karena lived in New York but traveled incessantly for her job.

"It's hot as hell," Noelle chimed glibly, then sat on the edge of the bed.

Karena chuckled. "Like it's not hot in Vegas."

"You've got that right," Noelle said as she smiled to herself. This is how it was with Karena, no matter what was bothering her, talking to Karena could always bolster her mood.

"So how's it going? I meant to call you last night but I got in late."

"Where are you now?"

"I'm home, thank God." Karena sighed. "This last trip was grueling. I'm telling you I'm going to need to train somebody to take over. I'm tired of all this running around."

"But you love your work."

"I love buying art, but I'm sick of traveling. I'd like to settle down in one place and just live for a while. I'm thinking of training Deena to do it."

Deena Lakefield was Karena's youngest sister and from all that Karena had told Noelle about her, she wasn't ready to take on such an important position.

"You sure about that?" Noelle asked. "You know how Deena is."

"Yeah, but it's about time she grew up, don't you think?"

"Hey, you know me. I'm the queen of needing to grow up. I can't even chime in on someone else's dilemmas with joining the adult world."

"But you did it. You've come a long way, Noelle. Even in the two years I've known you, I've seen your growth. Deena can do it. She just needs to put her mind to it."

"She needs the right motivation," Noelle added.

"Exactly. Now, stop changing the subject and answer my question. How are things going?"

"Well, I just got here, so there's really nothing to report." *Except that I've slept with the boss already.*

"How's the cousin? Is he just as good looking and intimidating as the rest of the Donovans?"

"Girl, please. You weren't even intimidated when you met Linc, Adam and Trent last summer."

"Sure I was. That's why I stayed near the grill. Henry Donovan is the only harmless one."

They both laughed at that one. Henry was Linc, Adam and Trent's father and he was charming and sweet and everything a girl would want in a father. Except he'd only had sons, but that hadn't stopped him from unofficially adopting Noelle as his daughter.

"Brock's not like the rest of the Donovans," she heard herself saying. "Don't get me wrong—he's definitely up to par in the looks department—but he has a more reserved attitude. A little too uptight for my tastes, though. Yeah, give me the in-your-face Trent any day."

"Hmm," Karena murmured.

"We're about to go tour the town and then we're heading over to the casino. I'll probably have to talk the entire time since he's so closed-lipped. That's a real headache, especially since we're supposed to be working together. But, hey, I'm not here to change the guy, just get the Gramercy II off the ground."

"But he looks good, right?" Karena interrupted.

Noelle's lips clamped shut as she thought about the question. She'd been so busy going through her list of why she didn't really like Brock, Karena's question had been a surprise. "Um, yeah. He's not bad to look at."

"And you're staying at his house?"

"That's right. Oh, the house is nice. It's big and has a lot of land. The pool is the best. I went for a swim this morning and then when Brock joined me we…" Noelle trailed off.

"Uh-huh, don't even try it," Karena warned. "I knew

there was more. I could hear it in your voice. You went for a swim and Brock joined you and then what?"

Noelle exhaled deeply. Okay, so she totally believed in signs. She'd been having a difficult time and the phone had rang. It had been Karena. She'd received the call for a reason. So with another deep breath, Noelle told Karena the rest and ended with, "I know. I know. I screwed up again. I can't believe it myself. You would think I'd learned my lesson by now."

"Stop doing that," Karena warned. "Luther was an ass, but you couldn't have predicted that the first time you met him."

"I could have waited to sleep with him. I could have gotten to know him better. Then I would have found out he was married a lot sooner."

"You found out he was married because one of his other mistresses thought it was time you knew. Luther makes a habit of cheating on his wife so he's used to perpetrating with the best of them. You can't blame yourself for that."

"Come on, Karena. I was poaching on another woman's property."

"I'm not denying that, Noelle. I'm just saying cut yourself some slack. There are women out there who poach and do it with a gleeful smile on their faces. But you're not one of them. You didn't know and when you found out, you kicked his tired behind to the curb. You did the right thing."

"He's still texting me, you know."

"See, that just shows that he's the one with the problem, not you. Now, back to Brock with the great lips and hands."

Noelle laughed. "That's enough details for you for one day. I've got to get going. He's probably waiting for me."

"I'll just bet he is."

"No. It's not going to be like that. Just like I told him this morning, it was a one-time deal. We did it and it's over. This is not how I want to work for Linc."

"You're a grown, good-looking woman and from what I'm hearing he's a grown, great-looking man. You both can do whatever you want and still get the job done for Linc."

"This isn't what I was sent here for. Besides, I don't know Brock and I'm not sure I want to get to know him. He's got secrets and issues of his own. I can tell by the way he broods and clams up whenever I start talking." Noelle was shaking her head. "No. It's best we keep this strictly business."

"If you say so," Karena finally added. "Well, if you don't want him, you know I've been going through my own drought."

"Don't play," Noelle said instantly defensive. "Didn't we just finish talking about poaching?"

Karena was laughing. "Yeah, but you don't want him. Right?"

Noelle smiled. Karena Lakefield was too smart for her own good. "Goodbye, Karena. I'll call you later in the week after I get settled."

"You sound like you're settled enough...on Brock, that is."

"Just business, Karena. That's all there is between me and Brock. Just business."

And as Noelle slipped her cell phone back into her

purse and left the room, she reminded herself of those words, putting the warmth growing in the pit of her stomach at the knowledge of seeing him again into one of her compartments, closing it off.

For good, she hoped.

Chapter 7

If she were aiming for the exact opposite of Las Vegas, there wasn't a better place than St. Michaels, Maryland. This quiet town seemed to be worlds away from the bright lights, chinking slot machines, rolling dice and piling chips that buzzed around her across the country. Instead, Noelle found herself walking down brick-paved streets lined with cozy cottages.

It put her in mind of Mayberry and *The Andy Griffith Show,* the twenty-first century version, of course. The streets were two way but small, and people milled about, townsfolk mixed with squads of tourists. The cutest little boating outfits hung in the bay window of a store called Chesapeake Bay Outfitters, while more eclectic items graced the windows and part of the sidewalk in front of a place named A Wish Called Wanda.

The sights and sounds were all so relaxing, so slow paced that Noelle found her steps slowing as she browsed. Never one to possess much patience, Noelle's shopping experience usually entailed bouncing in and out of stores grabbing up the first thing in sight she liked then moving on to the next. She hated keeping still and had been reprimanded more than a little bit by Grammy while she was growing up for just that reason.

"Energetic as five Energizer Bunnies," Jade used to say. Wouldn't her big sister laugh if she saw her taking time to stop at a shop, reach her hand into a bucket and feel the smoothness of a collection of colored seashells?

"How about a boat ride?" Brock asked, breaking Noelle's train of thought.

They hadn't spoken much since she'd come out of her room, dressed and ready to go. He'd been in the kitchen, drinking a cup of coffee and offered her one. Noelle was already jittery and on edge. Drinking coffee would have surely had her bouncing along the streets of St. Michaels, and that wasn't the image she wanted to project. So with mutual smiles, they'd set out for their tour.

Brock wanted her to feel the essence of the area, to help her get an idea of what guests they would be catering to. What Noelle had experienced so far was that the residents of St. Michaels might actually have the right idea—simply living their life. Maybe a casino was the last thing they needed.

"Sure, that sounds like fun. But do we have time? I mean, I don't want to be late for the meeting with Josette and Kent."

"We're fine. Besides, they'll wait."

He'd touched a hand to her elbow, then guided her

through the clusters of people on the small streets until
they came to a break in the shops. At his touch Noelle's
insides rippled. She'd been aware of his closeness all
morning but they hadn't touched, and that was a good
thing. Now her body was virtually on fire at something
as simple as his hand guiding her down the street. It was
embarrassing.

Deciding to keep focusing on her surroundings she
played the tourist, asking Brock questions. "I thought we
were going for a boat ride, but this looks like a restaurant."

"It is. They have the best steamed crabs here. We
should get some one night. You just cannot come to
Maryland and not enjoy some steamed crabs."

"So I've heard," she said with a smile. "But where's
the boat?"

"Be patient," Brock said. "I think there's something
else you'll like first." With that he grabbed her hand in
his and led her between the restaurant and what looked
like another souvenir shop.

Brock had been uncertain about how she'd act once
they were together, alone, again. However, Noelle was
acting like her normal cheerful self, initially. Then he'd
watched with a strange feeling growing inside as she'd
experienced the town and some of its attributes. As
she'd stopped and touched things he found himself
wanting to be what she touched. With every stroke of
her fingers over a seashell, a piece of clothing, Brock's
body tensed. Then when she stared at things such as
novelty clocks or key chains with the barest hint of a
smile on her face he'd felt a tightening in his chest that
was both foreign and alarming.

Still, the memory of that slight catch in her voice as

she left his room earlier this morning bothered him. Again, he knew he shouldn't wonder what had happened in her life to make her so sad after intercourse, but he couldn't help it. However, an hour later when she'd smiled at him and proclaimed she was ready for the meeting he figured asking her would be a mistake. So instead he'd opted to keep their time together, for the duration of the day, as business-like and unconfrontational as possible.

Noelle heard them before she actually saw them— the loud persistent quacking of ducks! Her gaze immediately went to the ground and what came waddling around the corner. Three beautifully colored ducks walked right on the street with her in single file as if that were the rule.

"Oh! Look at them. They're so pretty," she squealed, instantly kneeling to get a closer look.

The one had a black head with a bright orange beak. Its eyes were a darker shade of orange with a perfect black dot in the center. Its features were as sleek and shiny as that of a raven, its head held high as it pranced along the wood-planked ground.

Another one had a head in a shimmering emerald-green hue with a fierce streak of royal blue going down its backside, blending in with bark brown feathers. Its beak was yellow, its eyes dark, almost black. Their webbed feet carried them around, beaks opening each time they wished to speak.

Noelle was entranced. So much so that when Brock touched her shoulder, she jumped.

"Here. They're waiting for you to feed them," he told her, offering his hand to her.

Noelle instantly extended her hand and chuckled with glee as he dropped the small pellets into her palm. The ducks must have smelled them because now they waddled toward her. Lowering her arm she held out her hand and waited for them to come closer. As they did, all three of them, Brock knelt down beside her and hit the bottom of her hand so the pellets bounced out, scattering on the ground.

"They'll peck your arm off the way you're offering to all three of them," he said when she'd looked up at him with annoyance.

"Oh," she said, then looked back at the ducks happily milling about, pecking up the food.

It was back, he thought, that light in her eyes that touched a part of him Brock had long since closed off. He couldn't help but smile. "Come on."

He had her hand again and this time Noelle didn't focus on the heat. She watched the ducks until they were traveling so far down the wooden dock that she could barely see them.

Instead she saw what reminded her of an old tugboat. "Please tell me this is not what we're riding on."

"Can't do that," Brock said leading her to the boarding section ahead of him. "It'll be educational. This tour takes you down the Miles River, part of the Chesapeake Bay Estuary, which is the largest in the western hemisphere."

Yeah, that sounded educational, all right. For a moment Noelle wanted to ask what happened to the smiling Brock that had just helped her toss food at the ducks. But she refrained. It was, after all, a business trip.

So they set sail on the historic *Patriot,* she and Brock

taking seats on the upper deck. While she was more interested in the water, the banks that gave way to the greenest grass she'd ever seen and the palatial homes that were afforded this gorgeous view on a daily basis, Brock broke out into the position of historical guide. He told her things like why St. Michaels was known as The Town That Fooled The British for a skirmish during the War of 1812 and that here on the Miles River local watermen harvested clams, oysters and the famous Chesapeake Bay blue crab. All of which were probably facts of interest to the normal tourist.

But to Noelle it was simply jibberish. She wanted to see the people, to interact with them, to find out how living in such a beautifully serene place had affected their lives. In that way, she would know how to cater to them at the Gramercy II and quite possibly get some insight into how she could bottle up some of this serenity and take it back to Vegas with her come the end of the summer. Lord knows she needed it.

When the tour was over Noelle felt closer to nature than she ever had before. Probably not nature itself but the Miles River, thanks to the enchanting ride on the little tugboat that left her feeling happy and energized.

This morning's digression was far from her mind until they were walking along the dock and Brock suddenly swooped her into his arms.

"So did you enjoy the ride?" he was asking in that deep voice of his.

Noelle's palms flattened on his chest as she attempted to pull out of his grasp. As much as she liked St. Michaels and its beautiful views, she could not stand to be in Brock's arms. It was the one place where she had no control.

"Ah, I really liked it," she said, finally moving away from him.

He looked at her strangely, then let his arms fall to his sides. "Noelle, listen, about this morning," he began.

"No," she said, shaking her head. "This morning is over and done with. I don't want to talk about it anymore."

Brock looked as if he was going to argue with her, then simply switched gears. "Fine. Let's not be late for our meeting.

He'd oblige her for now, but they were going to talk. She could bet on that!

The building itself was beautiful. Steeped on top of a winding road that sloped down on the back end to meet the other side of the magnificent Miles River. The Gramercy II looked majestic yet simplistic in this small town setting.

"The architect did a great job capturing the ambiance of the Eastern Shore while still making a bold, contemporary statement," Noelle commented the moment they walked through the cooper-toned glass doors.

"Why thank you," a male voice responded.

Brock turned in the direction from which it had come, already extending his hand in greeting. "Kent Foster of Foster Designs meet Noelle Vincent from the Gramercy I."

Kent, a tall, slim man with skin the color of roasted pecans and eyes that sized and assessed, immediately shook his hand heartily while keeping his gaze on Noelle.

"Your design is simply beautiful," Noelle said as Kent took her hand. "It's a pleasure to meet you."

"The pleasure is definitely mine," Kent responded, bringing the back of Noelle's hand to his lips for a slow kiss.

Brock's jaw clenched.

Chapter 8

Kent Foster had an easy smile and cheerful demeanor. Brock had hired him five years ago to design his house. They'd been friends ever since.

"Where's Josette? I thought we were going to do the walk-through together," he said, willing his friend to let go of Noelle's hand this instant.

"She's around somewhere, making sketches and playing with her swatches. You know how she is with a blank canvas. So, Noelle, how's Brock treating you so far? When I heard you were going to stay with him instead of at one of the great bed-and-breakfasts in the area I was afraid for you. You know, Brock isn't the most personable host."

Brock shot Kent a warning look, then caught Noelle looking up at him. He tried to laugh it off but Kent was still holding her hand and she didn't look as if she minded at all.

This morning, she'd said what they'd done was over and they should both move on and for the moments after she'd said it Brock had felt confident that he could do just that. But after spending the morning with her he found that since he'd had a taste of her, his hunger had only increased. In addition to that basic hunger was something else that made Brock more than a little uncomfortable.

"He's been a wonderful host, helping me feed the ducks and everything," Noelle was saying, offering Brock a smile.

His *smile,* he thought and warmed instantly.

"Well, let's get this show on the road," Brock said, moving smoothly between Kent and Noelle, taking her hand from his friend's and twining her fingers in his own. He hoped she wouldn't pull away, yet the startled look in her eyes at his touch said she wasn't one hundred percent comfortable with it. "Call Josette on her cell," he said over his shoulder to Kent, who was grinning foolishly at him.

"Sure thing," Kent answered as they all moved to the first elevator.

Two hours later the foursome sat at the functional but ugly table and chairs that had been set up in what would soon be the blackjack area. From there they had a bird's-eye view of the rest of the room where more table games would be assembled.

"So what do you think, Noelle? Is it up to par with Vegas's rendition of the Gramercy?" Josette asked with her smoky voice.

Josette and Kent were the ultimate odd couple in

Brock's humble opinion. Kent was boisterous and fun-loving, and Josette was astute and clever, business-minded and serene. Kent was tall and thin, whereas Josette was much shorter, with a round frame that just bordered on chubby.

"This is different," Noelle began. "More sedate, a classical feel with a terrific historical backdrop. I think it will only enhance the Vegas facility by its differences. You guys have done a fantastic job."

Josette smiled warmly. "Thank you. Brock was worried about how you would perceive our small-town efforts, but I hoped you'd be a woman of vision. Glad to see my instincts were right."

"Las Vegas and Maryland are on two different scales of grandeur," Brock said in his defense. For a brief moment Noelle had looked a little stung by Josette's words. He hoped that his preconceived notions about her weren't offensive.

"I was a little leery at first myself. I mean, when Linc mentioned he wanted to open another casino and sent me out scouting for places, I stayed on the west coast, looking at equally fast-paced L.A. and Beverly Hills. I would have never considered this area. But I'm glad to see I was wrong."

If she was offended, she didn't show it. In fact, Brock was beginning to notice how upbeat and cordial she always seemed to be, except for those few moments in his room, this morning and then once they got off the boat. Those instances still had him puzzled, but for right now he'd take her smile.

"So, here are my design ideas for the VIP rooms and the public rooms. The gaming areas have a more classical casino look. But the waterfall in the center stage area will be the eye catcher."

Noelle flipped through the pictures Josette had given her. "That waterfall is going to be great. Have you seen the water show at Caesars Mall in Atlantic City? It's breathtaking. This is going to make that look like a wishing well," she said with a chuckle.

"Yes, I saw it and was inspired. I'm glad you like my twist on it." Josette practically beamed.

"Of course I do. Now, for the colors. I like the rich golds and muted champagnes. I'm thinking we could enhance those with a cranberry hue."

Leaning over the table, Josette moved through the swatches of fabric she had. "Hmm, I was thinking forest green."

"Yes, that might work, too," Noelle conceded as she felt the fabric in her hands. "But I think for the VIPs the red might seem more prominent, stately. If you know what I mean."

Josette was already nodding. "I do. I do. How about this?"

As the two women went on about their business Kent motioned for Brock to get up and walk with him. Brock obliged.

"She's beautiful" were Kent's first words when they were out of the women's earshot.

"She's competent," Brock responded. He didn't want Kent even thinking of Noelle along the lines of her looks.

Kent nodded. "And you're interested."

Brock frowned. "Interested in how this project is going to turn out, yes."

"Don't try to play me, Brock. I've known you for a while now and I've never seen you watch a woman the way you've been watching her all afternoon. Everywhere she moves, every word she says, you're right there hanging on to it as if it were spoken by Queen Elizabeth."

"If you really knew me, you'd know I don't give a flying fig about Queen Elizabeth."

Kent laughed. "But you're definitely feeling Noelle Vincent. Hey, man, it's okay. I can't blame you. She's fine as hell. If I weren't already married, I'd definitely try to get with her."

"I'm a grown man. I'm too old to try to get with anybody."

"You know what I mean. And she's staying at your house. All I'm saying is you've got it made." He clapped Brock on his back before returning to the women.

Noelle looked up as Kent sat down then around the man until she caught his gaze. She smiled briefly then went back to talking with Josette again.

If Kent only knew.

While it would appear that this was a great opportunity, Brock was beginning to rethink it. Especially after this morning.

The sex had been fast and hot and the best he'd ever had in his life. A small part of him wanted to think it was more, but Noelle had effectively doused that flame with her parting words. They weren't going to tell Linc because it wasn't going to happen again, that was her summation.

Brock still wasn't sure how he felt about that or what he was going to do about it. But for right now he needed to keep his friend focused on business and not on Noelle because he swore if Kent looked at her with that hungry look in his eye one more time, he'd be going home with that eye blackened.

Chapter 9

"Do you want to have some dinner?" Brock asked when he and Noelle had finally returned to his house.

The afternoon with Josette and Kent had drawn out because they'd gone to Josette's office and looked at even more materials and talked more about the casino layout, specifically the décor of the rooms in the VIP section as these would be the first in the Gramercy II Tower to open.

So it was well after seven in the evening when they returned.

"I'm pretty pooped. That great big seafood buffet we visited for lunch has managed to keep me feeling full."

Brock watched her as he'd been doing all day. Every wave of her hand, toss of her head, blink of her eye, seemed to be an act of purposeful languidness. Her legs stretched on for miles and miles so when he watched her walk he was entranced by the long strides she took.

When she talked her hands always moved, in sort of an animated gesture, but one that kept him attentive to every word she spoke. She always looked at whomever she was speaking to, eye to eye, as if they were the only person in the room. It was sort of intense for a guy used to being alone and doing business on the mildly cold perspective. Yet, it made Brock seem just a little more important than normal.

"Well, I'm going to fix a sandwich. Otherwise I'll be up in the middle of the night, making enough noise to wake the dead while I search for something."

"Suit yourself," she said with a shrug.

"Actually, if you join me, that would suit me just fine."

She hesitated and he knew in that moment she was preparing her defenses. Since his attempt earlier this afternoon, she'd successfully ignored this subject.

Something told him she could probably continue this way for the rest of the summer. By this way, he meant not discussing the fact that just this morning they'd had sex. He wondered if she handled everything in her life by ignoring it. Sex aside, her words before she'd left him alone had Brock perplexed. Noelle Vincent did not strike him as a woman with an identity crisis. So saying this wasn't who she was bothered him. While he in no way fooled himself to believe that this was some fated love connection, possibly because that was the last thing he was looking for, he still felt that this warranted some discussion. Agreeing not to tell Linc wasn't their only issue. Figuring out how they would proceed through the rest of this project was another one.

"Come on, you don't have to eat. You can just keep me company."

He'd turned without waiting for a response from her but was pleased to hear that she was following behind him into the kitchen.

Brock was getting out lunch meats and lettuce from the refrigerator, then moved to the counter to get the bread. "What are you thinking?" he asked when he caught her watching him with an amused stare.

"I'm thinking that it's a wonder you stay so fit with your appetite. You had three plates of food this afternoon and now you're fixing what definitely looks like the beginnings of a Dagwood Bumstead sandwich and I'm just amazed that you aren't sporting a potbelly or at the very least a spare tire around your waist."

Brock chuckled. "I like to eat. I offset that habit with a lot of physical exercise."

She nodded as if she already knew that. "Why don't you have a home gym? Linc has two in his house and I didn't see a gym when we were in town earlier."

"Linc's always been sort of obsessed with the body-building thing. Actually, no, I think it started out more as a competition with him and Trent. Me, on the other hand, I prefer physical labor."

"Is that why you got into construction?"

"I've always liked to build things," he responded. "I like creating something from nothing." What Brock didn't say was that his father had introduced him to the world of building.

"So you always knew you wanted to be a builder. That's nice."

"What's nice? Being a builder?"

"No. Always knowing what you wanted to do with your life."

"I take it you didn't set out to be a casino manager?"

"No. That was the furthest thing from my mind."

"Let me guess?" He put his sandwich down and stared at her with a half smile. "You wanted to be a model."

"Of course not. That was further from my mind than casino manager."

"Why? I'd say you definitely have the looks for it." She didn't blush, nor did she acknowledge the compliment.

"Maybe so. But I don't have the patience. Standing still while somebody takes my picture or tells me which way to stand, which way to look, is not my cup of tea. I've never been that disciplined."

With his sandwich complete Brock filled a glass with juice and sat across from her at the island. "So how'd you end up managing Linc's casino?"

"Hmph, that's a long, funny story."

He took a drink from his glass, then lifted his sandwich and tilted his head toward her. "Go ahead, I've got time."

Making herself comfortable on the stool across from him, Noelle propped her elbows up on the marble countertop. "I like shoes," she began.

Brock paused midbite, giving her a quizzical stare.

"Okay. It's a fetish. I absolutely love shoes. And because of that character flaw I sort of became caught up in the casinos and ended up owing money. Because I was gainfully unemployed at the time I went to my sister to bail me out, once again. Only this time, Jade didn't even have the money. Her jackass ex-fiancé had cleaned her bank account out when he'd split. So in an effort to help me, because that's how Jade is, she went to the casino to try and win back the money that I owed.

Instead she ended up losing, causing us both to owe even more money. Luckily she and Linc had a history and were able to work out a payment plan."

Brock laughed. "Oh, yeah, the date he bought for a week. I remember that."

"The date that became his wife and the mother of his children," Noelle added.

"Who would have guessed that an arrangement like that could end up the way it did?"

She drummed her nails on the counter. "I know. It seems beyond weird for Jade to walk into a casino and instead of coming out with a fortune, she came out with a future. But I couldn't be happier for her and for Linc. They're meant to be together."

"You believe in love, marriage, meant to be together and all that jazz?"

"I believe in love. I believe in commitment. So when two people find that they can share those things, then yes, I believe they should go for it."

That was interesting. It wasn't as if Brock didn't believe in those things, as well, but in his position, love and commitment weren't going to be enough. "You speak as if you've never experienced those things."

She nodded. "I haven't."

"Do you want to?"

Here it was, the moment she'd known was coming. It had been too much to think he wouldn't venture toward this discussion again. She stopped tapping and stared at him evenly. "Look, there's no need for you to get nervous. I'm not the type of girl that believes that sex equals a commitment. We're attracted to each other and, just like I said this morning, we acted on it. It's over and done now so you don't have to worry about me making it into something else."

Brock picked up his napkin and wiped his mouth. "That's good to know. So now what? We had a one night stand and we continue to work together like nothing happened?"

"Well, Mr. Remington, I'll give you this. You're not easily forgotten," she said pointedly. Just because she had no intention of sleeping with him again didn't mean she couldn't at least be honest about the experience.

"Well, Ms. Vincent, I'll give you the same compliment," he replied genuinely.

She wasn't easily forgotten and she wasn't exaggerating when she said she could never be a model because she couldn't keep still very long. She was already slipping off the stool, going to the cabinet and reaching for a glass, he suspected to fix something to drink. Either that or she was trying to put some distance between them and this conversation.

But Brock had no intention of letting her off that easily. "So we've already discussed that we're not going to tell Linc. And now we've accepted that we're attracted to each other. We both equally enjoyed the sex."

She'd gone to the refrigerator and taken out a carton of orange juice. Pouring a glass full she said, "Correct."

"Now, my next question is…" Brock paused, waited for her to put the orange juice back in the refrigerator and face him again.

"When do we get to enjoy the sex again?"

She almost choked.

Coughing and covering her mouth with one hand Noelle gingerly placed the glass down on the counter.

She'd known this was a mistake. They'd almost made it successfully through the day without touching this subject. And had she simply gone straight to bed as originally planned she would not be standing in front of him with his dark eyes tearing into her calm facade.

One thing Noelle had noticed about Brock Remington in the hours spent working with him today was that he was tenacious. From the heated discussions with city hall regarding the gaming permits to the debate with Josette over the cost of the carpets she'd selected, he was a man that bargained until the very end.

Fortunately for her this wasn't a situation that could be negotiated. Noelle's mind was made up and her decision had nothing to do with Brock directly. The fact that their attraction was so strong that she'd momentarily forgotten her resolve when it came to relationships and men was unfortunate but she could fix it. She had to.

"Haven't you ever heard of a one night stand?" she asked, trying valiantly to keep this as light as possible.

"I have and I've participated in them a time or two. But I get the distinct impression what we shared was a bit more than that."

"No." She shook her head negatively, even though her body was humming to his words. That same intrinsic feeling she'd gotten when he'd walked her to her room and kissed her and then when he'd joined her in the pool. It was like his words, his voice alone could summon a part of her that she had no control over. And that was just too damn weird to comprehend. "It was just a one night stand, Brock. You don't know me and I don't know you. In fact, we both should have exercised a little more self-control. I'm sure this isn't what Linc had in mind for us working together."

"Linc has nothing to do with this. This wasn't about the casino."

"But it is. I'm only here because of the casino. Otherwise you and I would have never met."

"We would have met at Trent's wedding or some other family function."

"Not necessarily. You weren't at Linc or Adam's wedding, nor were you at the twins' christening. So it's logical that we could have gone even longer without meeting."

"Logistics and excuses. I'm asking you frankly if we'll be having sex again."

Sexy as hell and just as candid as she was with her words. She had to admire that regardless of the situation. "No. We won't," she said just as candidly, then walked out of the room.

He didn't call after her, nor did he follow her, which was a relief. But as Noelle took the steps two at a time, in a hurry to get as far away from him and her still-burning desire for him as quickly as possible, she wondered if that was truly the end of this conversation. Or if, like her own body, Brock's would demand that he continue to push her.

Lord, she hoped not. Because as strong and focused as Noelle claimed to be now, there was no denying that something about Brock Remington had her stirred up. Something she was afraid her heart couldn't handle.

Chapter 10

"Good morning," Brock said when Linc came on the line. He was sitting in his office, leaning back against his chair, his long legs propped up on the end of the desk, crossed at his ankles. The speakerphone was on so his hands were free.

The conference call was at the same time every Wednesday morning. It had been for the last six weeks. The routine hadn't changed, Brock surmised. Only the situation had.

"Hey. So how are things going?" That was always Linc's first question, designed to lead into a summary of all of last week's happenings with the Gramercy II.

This morning Brock hesitated.

"Brock? Man, you there?"

"Ah, yeah. I'm here." Brock reached for the folder on his desk, trying to get his thoughts together. Which was easier said than done since in the last two days his mind had done a complete three-sixty turn from the Gramercy II to the sexy little site manager. Not to mention the fact that he wanted her again and she was hell-bent on keeping their relationship strictly business.

Noelle, he sighed, having been unable to get her, her name, her body out of his mind. After their tryst she'd been as thrown off-kilter as he was. Yet she'd surprised him by not acting hysterical either way. She wasn't apologetic and she wasn't angry. She'd simply accepted and moved on.

"I was going to ask you how things were working out with Noelle. Jade said she talked to her for a few minutes Monday night. She said you two were getting along."

Brock cleared his throat, having just realized that he must have said her name aloud. "Noelle's great," he answered quickly. "I mean, she certainly knows her job. We met with Kent and Josette yesterday and she and Josette really seemed to hit it off. I think we'll be able to proceed on schedule."

"Good. Noelle really takes pride in her work so I have no doubt she'll do well. How are we coming on the additional permits you said you needed?"

"Does she have a boyfriend?" Brock heard himself asking instead.

"What? Who?"

"Noelle. Does she have a boyfriend back in Vegas?"

For a moment Linc was quiet. "Not that I know of. I mean, at least not anymore. Should I even ask why you want to know?"

"No. It's nothing. I was just asking because she's a pretty woman. I figured there would have to be some-one in her life missing her while she's all the way out here working for the next few months." And if there was, how was he going to react to that fact?

"Uh-huh," Linc said.

"Let's get back to the gaming permits," Brock said, cursing to himself for even bringing that personal question about Noelle into this business conversation. "It's June now, and everything should be in no later than the first of August. By Labor Day weekend we should be up and rolling as planned."

Brock continued to rattle on about permits and casino business while Linc simply listened. When he'd finally come to the end of his updates, he asked, "So is all that cool with you?"

"Don't touch her," Linc warned in a tone that Brock didn't hear him use often.

"What?"

"I said, don't touch her. I don't care how good you think she looks, how attractive you might think she is, Noelle is off-limits. She's been through a lot in her young life and the last thing she needs is a summer affair."

"And you think I'm looking for a summer affair?"

Linc paused. "I don't know what you're looking for, Brock. What I do know is that women are a dime a dozen to you. I remember a time when they were for me, too. You take your time, but when you decide on one you proceed full speed ahead. So I'm just warning you not to decide on Noelle."

"Linc, she's an adult. She can make her own decisions."

"She's my wife's sister. You have no idea what I'll have to go through if you mess with her. And she's like a kid sister to me, so don't go there."

"She's not your kid sister by blood and you and I

aren't blood relatives." The moment Brock said it he knew it was a mistake. The Donovans had done nothing to him but accept him with open arms. Taking his anger about the situation with his parents out on them wasn't called for. "That's not what I meant. I apologize," he said quickly, because that's the type of man he was. If he was wrong, he owned up to it.

"I can't believe that still bothers you."

"It doesn't," Brock insisted, pinching the bridge of his nose. Apparently, along with his new houseguest fresh feelings about what happened to his parents all those years ago were back. Not that they ever stayed gone for long anyway. That had been a painful time in Brock's life, a time that he relived year after year. Having Noelle here could have been a buffer, but instead he felt as if the wound was open and fresh once more.

"That's an obvious lie. Look, I don't know much about what happened with your parents—Uncle Albert and Aunt Darla thought that was your personal business. But if you ever want to talk about it, I'm here."

Clearing his throat, Brock replied, "Nah, I'm cool."

"Then just know that outside of our familial connections I'm very protective of Noelle because it seems like she attracts every bum that walks the Earth. Not that you're remotely in that category, but I'm just tired of seeing her go through so much because of the men she chooses to date."

Brock was rubbing his fingers over his chin, thinking about Linc's words. "I hear you. Nobody likes to go through a lot of unnecessary drama."

"And Noelle has had more than her share. So just take it easy with her."

Brock laughed. "Hey, it's me you're talking to, not Trent."

Linc had no choice but to join in on that laughter. "Man, you should see him with Tia. He can't wait until she has that baby so he can marry her. I'm telling you I never thought I'd see the day."

"I know. When I heard, I couldn't believe it. I felt like all my bachelor mentors were gone."

"That's right, you are younger than us. But you wait, one day you'll take that plunge, too."

"No," Brock said with finality. "I won't. Marriages don't last in my family. Things go bad and change for the worst and there are always casualties."

"You weren't a casualty, Brock. You were their son and I'm sure if they could have changed the outcome of the situation they would have. Sometimes things just happen and we have no choice but to roll with the punches."

"Yeah?"

"Yeah. And I think you ended up with a pretty good life regardless. You're a success, your business is a success. You came into our family just in time for me and Trent to team up with you and Adam to kick your butts in spades, too."

Another chuckle and Brock was appreciating his connection with the Donovans once more. "Now you're dreaming. You and Trent never kicked our butts. Now, Bailey and Brandon, they can play a mean hand. Something about that twin connection they have," Brock said, thinking of his adopted twin sister and brother.

"True. So true," Linc chimed in. "Hey, what's going on with those two? Brandon was here a couple of months ago, talking about this fancy new job he's got in Houston. But I haven't heard anything about Bailey."

"I talked to Brandon about two weeks ago. He's loving the new job at TJB Investments. In fact, he's doing such a good job his boss, I think his name is Ty Braddock, has given him even more responsibilities. It seems Braddock and his wife have just had a baby and he wants to spend some time at home with them. As for Bailey, I'm surprised Trent didn't tell you the job he worked out for her."

"Trent? What's he doing for Bailey? You know those two mix like oil and water."

Brock laughed remembering the heated arguments between the two cousins who had opposite views on everything from the weather to politics. "I know. But as soon as Trent got wind of the fact that Bailey was looking to go into law enforcement, he stepped in. Said he wasn't about to have her carrying guns and running loose on innocent citizens. He got her a job with his new PI firm."

"So Bailey's in L.A. with Trent?"

"Nah, like you said the two of them don't mix. She was looking for a change of scenery and was actually considering heading out east to maybe work with the FBI in D.C. She's still thinking about that but in the meantime Trent put her in his east-coast office with, what's his partner's name out there?"

"Sam Desdune," Linc offered.

"Yeah, that's him. She's pushing papers here for their east-coast cases, doing strictly office stuff until Sam and Trent think she's ready for more heavy-duty work. Which, since we both know how protective Trent is of the womenfolk in the family, will be ten minutes after never."

Linc laughed along with Brock. "That's the truth. But I'm glad she's spreading her wings a little. Uncle Albert had been kind of keeping her close since Aunt Darla's death."

"I know," Brock said, not really wanting to relive the sadness of another lost loved one.

"So, all right, get moving on the casino. Jade and I will be there in September for the opening."

"Cool. It'll be ready."

"And, Brock," Linc said solemnly.

"Yeah?"

"Remember what I said about Noelle. She's been through a lot. I don't want her hurt again."

"Don't worry about it. I'm not in the business of hurting women," Brock responded.

An hour after he'd disconnected with Linc, Brock was still thinking about his cousin's words. So Noelle had been through a lot, she was attracted to bums. All that spelled out drama to Brock, the one thing he didn't need more of in his life. Linc didn't have to warn him anymore—what he'd told him alone should keep Brock away from her.

However, the attraction was there, thick and intense. So much so that they'd already acted on it and he'd even tried for a second round. But Noelle didn't seem to want that. As attracted to each other as they still were, Noelle had left him hanging in the kitchen last night, effectively killing the idea of another round in bed with her.

In fact, she'd moved so fast to get away from him he would have thought it hilarious had he not seen the moment her eyes grew leery.

This had been the second time he'd sensed this other side of her, this softer more vulnerable side than the bravado she always put forth. The first had been just before she'd left him in the bedroom. For a moment he'd thought she was afraid of him or what had happened between them. But that just didn't seem right. The last thing he would associate with Noelle Vincent was fear. She didn't seem to know the meaning of that word. Yet something had her shaken. Now Brock knew that was most likely something from her past, something he should probably steer clear of.

The only problem with that assumption was the overwhelming need he felt to be near her, to make her smile and keep her smiling.

With a sigh, Brock wondered what he'd gotten himself into by not reigning in his desire for the vivacious stranger. Initially he'd been worried about her coming out here and hampering the project. Instead, she was wreaking havoc on his body, his thoughts and the position he'd taken with women all his life.

Brock wasn't the marrying type and even though Noelle had assured him their one night stand was over and done with, she'd also admitted to believing in love and happy endings.

She believed that one day she'd find both those things. But this was not the day and Brock was not the one to give them to her. So, yes, it was best that he take Linc's advice and not touch her again. It was best for him and for Noelle.

Now if he could only convince his traitorous body of his decision.

Chapter 11

Sitting on the deck as the sun beamed down in the early afternoon, Claudette Simmons flipped through the latest edition of *Mega Explosion* magazine. It was a magazine dedicated to all news in the gaming industry. She read them because her father had always read them, and he'd done so because he was fascinated with the inner workings of casinos. So much so that he threw each of his paychecks away by gambling.

Claudette had a better way to spend her money, she thought with a smile and a gaze at the eighteen-karat flawless diamond on her left hand. That was her latest gift from her husband, Luther, the lying, conniving bastard that he was. Still, his bank account and tireless dedication to keeping her in the lifestyle to which she'd grown accustomed kept her with him.

At least that had been her frame of mind until she'd

received that package last night. The pictures burst into her mind and she cringed. Sure, Claudette had known her husband was a philanderer—that's how she'd met him. Usually Luther's affairs were on the down low. She knew, of course, because she had a private investigator on retainer for his cheating ass. That was a pro-active measure on her behalf. Divorce accounted for the demise of three out of four marriages in the U.S. Claudette was no fool. She planned to stay ahead of the game and keep everything she could in the event that her union with Luther went downhill.

Something she sensed was about to happen.

Besides, he was embarrassing her now. By being seen publicly with his mistress. That brought her name into his scandalous behavior and that was not allowed. She just needed to figure out a good way to hit his ass hard. No, she wasn't going to divorce him just yet. But she wanted to bring him to his knees to show him that he'd finally met his match.

As she sipped her coffee and continued to flip through the pages of the magazine, her mind buzzed with options. Then she saw it.

It was her. The girl in the pictures with Luther. She'd never known any of Luther's mistresses' names, never cared to, until now.

Multimillionaire Lincoln Donovan will unveil his second casino coming this Labor Day on Maryland's scenic Eastern Shore. This one-hundred-million-dollar project is being headed up by Brock Remington of Remington Construction and Noelle Vincent, sister-in-law to Lincoln Donovan and manager of the renowned Gramercy I in Las Vegas.

So Luther's new toy was related to the reputable Donovans, she realized after reading the article. Rubbing a long, manicured nail over the picture, Claudette's mind began to click. The girl was pretty enough. Well, her mouth was too wide, her eyes filled with a childish gleam, but she had great hair and a pretty, clear complexion. The picture of the woman standing next to Lincoln Donovan was a waist-up shot, but Claudette could see enough to know that she possessed the curves that Luther preferred.

"Interesting," Claudette whispered. "Very interesting indeed."

The next week flew by with Brock spending most of his time in his office, dealing with issues about materials and fighting to get the gaming permits on time.

He'd seen Noelle mostly in passing because she and Josette had been working nonstop on the VIP rooms. He remembered a note she'd scrawled and stuck to the refrigerator a day or two ago about lighting and needing to sit down with him to go over floor plans and structural points, but Brock hadn't found a spare moment. Which was sort of on purpose. Brock figured the less time they were actually in each other's presence, the easier it would be to get over this desire for her. That, unfortunately, wasn't working.

Until tonight.

It had been a very long day, one that he'd been dreading since this time last year, one he would continue to dread for the rest of his life. It was his birthday.

Looking at his watch as he stuck his key into the door of his house, Brock saw that it was just a little after eight. He wondered if Noelle was still awake. Maybe she was what he needed tonight. They could talk if she was around. Brock liked talking to Noelle, although he had to admit, he didn't want to talk about business. He'd had enough of that for the time being. And while he'd been doing his damnedest to steer clear of her, today she'd been on his mind a lot.

She shouldn't have been, that was certainly true. She'd made herself perfectly clear regarding their moment of indiscretion and she'd seemed anything but brokenhearted over it. So there was really no valid reason why he couldn't leave well enough alone. There were millions of men all over the world who longed for a woman to take one moment of highly satisfying sex as nonchalantly as Noelle apparently had. However, Brock was finding it a bitter pill to swallow.

Aside from that, he really liked spending time with Noelle. That morning they'd spent touring St. Michaels had been one of the most relaxing and fun times he'd ever spent with a member of the opposite sex who he wasn't related to in some way. Knowing she would be home when he arrived and there in the morning when he awoke was comforting on some level because he'd never had that type of companionship before. Surely there wasn't any harm in enjoying it while it lasted. If there was he was too tired to think about it right now.

Letting himself into the house and closing the door behind him, Brock crossed the small foyer and headed directly into the living room, hoping Noelle would be there. Flicking on the lights, he saw, with disappointment, that she wasn't. Walking through the front end of the house didn't produce her, either.

So he was heading to the kitchen to get himself a snack and then off to bed when he thought to check the porch. The moment he stepped through the threshold of the enclosed unit to the side of his house the lights switched on and three voices yelled, "Surprise!"

Across the room they stood, Kent with a drink in his hand, Josette with a cake and enough candles that once lit would surely start a small fire, and Noelle with a blue Mylar balloon with *Happy Birthday* scrawled over it.

"Surprise, indeed," Brock said, sending a warning glare to Kent.

"Don't shoot daggers at me, man. I tried to tell them this was a bad idea. I told them you didn't celebrate your birthday and that you wouldn't like us trying to, either. I told you, didn't I?" Kent took another sip of his drink after nodding to his wife.

"Yes. He told us," Noelle offered, moving closer to Brock. "And I told him it was ridiculous. Everybody's given one day in their life to celebrate something as simple as living. So you're not allowed to pass that up. It would be like…blasphemy or something." With an outstretched arm, she offered the balloon to Brock.

"Happy birthday," she said sweetly.

Had they been alone and she'd offered him the silly looking balloon and that gorgeous smile of hers, Brock might have been inclined to let his negative feelings about today go. But with Kent giving him a knowing grin and Josette putting the cake on the table and flicking the lighter to each candle, he just felt more irritated.

"Thanks," he said through clenched teeth.

"Come on, we've ordered dinner and Josette had this great cake made for you. Surely you can withstand a little celebration." Noelle had grabbed him by the hand and was pulling him toward the table.

"Of course, I can," he told her. But he wouldn't like it. Kent knew he wouldn't like it and he knew why. This was the day of his birth, yes, but it was also the day his father had died and his mother had lost her mind. It was not a day Brock wished to commemorate at all.

So the threesome sang "Happy Birthday" with Kent slightly off tune and Noelle sounding as if she'd grown up in the church choir. She sat beside him as they ate, she and Josette keeping up pleasant conversation the entire time.

An hour later, Brock thought he'd finally reached his limit when Kent handed him an envelope.

"Just a little something from the missus and myself," he said with a chuckle.

Brock didn't frown but he did look at Kent sternly. His demeanor had been precarious since he'd arrived, Noelle noticed. It had been Josette that mentioned to-day being Brock's birthday and Kent who vehemently opposed of them doing anything. But in the end Noelle's power of persuasion had worked because she firmly believed that each and every living person should cele-brate the day of their birth for the simple fact that they weren't promised another one.

"You didn't have to do this," she heard Brock say, and wondered why it was so hard for him to accept these small acts of kindness.

"We know," Josette said, reaching a hand across the table to touch the one of his that had just put his napkin down. "But we wanted to."

Giving her hand a light squeeze, Brock opened the

envelope and pulled out what looked like tickets. "It's for a European cruise," he announced.

"Wow! That should be a great vacation," Noelle said, hoping that would at least cheer him up a little. Never had she seen anybody look so down about a birthday cake and dinner.

"There's two tickets and an open sail date," he said, eyeing Kent.

"Just in case you don't want to travel alone. And I know you're not going to even consider leaving until after the casino is finished."

"It'll be a great way for you to unwind after all your hard work," Josette added.

With a heaviness in his chest that he hadn't expected, Brock thanked them, the two closest people to him besides his adopted family.

"And now, the celebration is officially over," Kent said, coming to his feet.

Brock stood as Kent clapped him on the shoulder. "Don't be too angry. Remember, she doesn't know," he whispered as Noelle and Josette started to clean the table.

"I'm not angry," he said. How could he be when she'd given him a balloon and his special smile and Kent and Josette had given him a cruise?

"No. But you're not happy, either."

"Happiness is overrated. I've told you that before," he said, then turned to take the dishes from Josette's hands. "Don't worry about this. I'll clean up. You and Kent go on home. You've got a long drive back to Easton."

Letting him take the dishes, Josette came up on her tiptoes and kissed Brock's cheek. "You've got to let go sometime, Brock. Why not now?"

Accepting her words and the well meaning behind them, Brock smiled down at Josette. "Thanks. I'll be all right."

Noelle watched the exchange with mounting questions. Clearly something had happened to him on this day, something that he didn't like to talk about but that kept him from finding the smallest enjoyment in the day of his birth.

She shouldn't ask. She shouldn't care.

She didn't, Noelle decided and continued to clear the table. She heard the front door close and was about to go out to get the rest of the dishes when Brock met her in the kitchen, his hands full of glasses and cake plates.

"I was going to get that," she said.

"It's okay. I'm used to cleaning up after myself."

He didn't sound angry like he did when he'd first come home, but he didn't sound chipper, either. "Well, it's your birthday so you don't have to do it. Why don't you go ahead and go to bed? I'll take care of this."

For endless moments he only stood there staring at her. Noelle wanted to reach out to him, to touch his cheek in offer of comfort. She wanted to help him through his pain, which was more than idiotic of her. They weren't friends and they weren't family. They were working together. This urge she felt to comfort him was ridiculous and probably only a result of the intimacy they'd so foolishly shared.

So she turned away from him, before she'd been forced to do something like hug him or, even worse, hold him. Picking up the dishwashing liquid, she squirted an enormous amount into the sink, then held back a sneeze as she turned on the water and the floral scent wafted up to her nose.

"I have some work to do," he said from behind her.

"Okay," she said stiffly.

"Thank you," he said, clearing his throat. "For tonight, I mean. Kent and Josette would have never done this on their own. So I know it had to be your idea."

She shrugged. "I like birthdays, so sue me."

She liked birthdays and feeding ducks and swimming. All information that shouldn't amount to a hill of beans for him, but did.

Chapter 12

With each step taken Noelle argued with herself. It wasn't any of her business. If he wanted to brood and stew on his birthday, so be it. But if he was hurting and needed someone to talk to, she couldn't really walk away. Could she?

"You spend too much time alone," Noelle said, leaning against the doorjamb of his office where she'd found him behind the desk an hour after dinner.

"I like my life just the way it is, thank you," he snapped, barely looking up at her.

"Well, excuse me for being concerned," she retorted, then turned to leave.

At her tone Brock looked up. She'd changed from the slacks and blouse she'd worn at dinner. Her long hair was pulled back into a ponytail. She wore denim shorts and a tank top that was cut too low for decency.

"Noelle?"

"What?" she answered tightly without turning back to face him.

"I'm sorry."

She turned slowly in what Brock thought had to be the sexiest move short of her undressing right then and there. "I'm used to being alone. I usually like it that way," he offered.

"It's not healthy, but if it's your preference, so be it. I won't disturb you."

"No." He stood. "It's not my preference. I mean, at least not while you're here."

She folded her arms over her chest and simply stared at him. "There's something about you, Brock Remington. Something going on in your head that you refuse to share with anyone. I think it's something painful that you don't know how to deal with yourself."

Because she was way too close to the truth, Brock walked toward her. "You know what I like to do when I'm alone?"

Her lips quirked. "What? And don't tell me it involves hand lotion."

Brock chuckled. *She could do that to him,* he thought suddenly. When he was out of sorts or just in a bad mood, she could make him laugh. He'd never had anyone that could do that for him. "No, and get your mind out of the gutter. I like to play checkers."

He didn't know why he was telling her this, but as he made his way to the cabinet, opened the door and pulled out the older game, it just felt right.

"My dad taught me how to play."

"Really?" she asked, stepping farther into his office. "I'd never peg Albert Donovan for a checkers player."

Brock sat the game down on the table near the window and looked pointedly at her. "Albert's not my real father."

Noelle was across the table from him now, opening the box. "I know. Jade told me that he and his late wife adopted you after your parents died. So technically he is your father now."

Brock took a deep, steadying breath. "Twenty-one years ago today my father died and I went to live with Albert and Darla."

"Oh, Brock, I'm sorry. That's why you didn't want a celebration?"

"I don't like to remember the day, the feelings," he said simply.

He continued, "Don't get me wrong. I appreciate everything that Albert and Darla did for me. I couldn't have asked for a better upbringing and I will love Albert forever for his sacrifice."

Noelle was already shaking her head. "I don't think it was a sacrifice for him. Albert seems like a really loyal man, like the rest of the Donovan men. If your father was his close friend, of course he'd do whatever he could to take care of his son."

"You think it's as simple as that?" he asked, noting she'd already pulled out the board and was setting up the red pieces as her own. Red suited her feisty nature and almost made him smile.

"Sure it is. I'm grateful to Linc and the Donovans for all they've done for me. I love them for opening their arms to me and to Jade. They've earned my loyalty, so whatever it is they need, if I could provide it I would, without a second thought."

And at that moment Brock realized her words were absolutely true. She was loyal and caring and genuine, traits he hadn't seen in many women.

He sat down in the chair across from her. He set up his pieces and they began to play. She didn't talk a lot through the game, which was different because Noelle always seemed to have something to say. He'd noticed that about her in the two weeks she'd been here. She talked to everyone she met as if she'd known them all her life. She was curious by nature and dangerously smart. Her laughter was quick and contagious, her smile alluring and satisfying. All clear and upfront, just like her. With Noelle it seemed what you saw was what you got. She was refreshing.

So much so that Brock found himself relaxing. "My mother didn't die," he said suddenly when she had two kings to his three but was giving him a sound run for his money.

"What happened to her?"

"She took sick. After my father died." Brock thought about his words then corrected them, "No. She became sick before he died."

"Where is she now?"

"Delancie Psychiatric Center," he replied as easily as if he were answering a question about the weather.

Noelle did look up at him then. "Do you visit her?"

"I haven't in a long while," he replied, feeling her gaze burning against him but refusing to look up. He moved one of his kings into a corner spot and waited for her.

"Were you and she close?"

"Yeah."

"How long's it been since you've seen her?"

"About two years."

"Two years. Huh." She moved her piece without thought. Brock jumped her and took her king. "You should go and see her," she said.

Brock looked at her then. "Why?"

"Because she's your mother." She waited a beat, then said, "And you miss her."

"She left me," Brock grumbled, then looked away.

"When she got sick, you mean?"

"Either way, it doesn't matter. She left. My father was gone and then she was gone and I moved to Texas."

"She can't help that she's sick, Brock."

"You don't know that. You don't know her."

"No. I don't. But I do know what it feels like to not have a mother at all. My mother drank herself to death because my deadbeat father couldn't be a man. My grandmother raised Jade and me and she was everything to us. When she died, I was devastated because I felt like she'd left me just like my mother and my father had. But then I realized that she hadn't left—her job was completed and I was being selfish for thinking otherwise."

She stood, looking down at him. "I don't take you for a selfish person, Brock. And I don't know what happened with your mother. But what I do know is that sometimes people do things because it's their destiny, not their choice. You should think about that before you rush to judge her."

Their game was over, and he'd shared enough. So why did he still want her to stay? Why did he desperately want to explain to her how he felt? So she'd approve, so she wouldn't be looking at him with barely masked pity in her eyes.

"It's not like you think. There was a scandal. My parents were what you'd call the Romeo and Juliet of their time. My mother's family was from a long line of blue bloods up north in Maine. My father was from here. He met her while on a business trip when he started his first construction company. They wanted to be married right away. Her parents disapproved, said she was marrying beneath her. My father's parents were insulted and forbid him to marry my mother, as well."

She'd taken her seat again and was watching him attentively. Her eyes were alight, but with concern this time, genuine interest in what it was he said.

"They married anyway and my mother moved here. When my father's company began to do well they hired a maid to help my mother around the house. They didn't know that the maid really worked for my mother's father. He, apparently, was incensed by the scandal my mother marrying my father had brought to his family, so he'd decided to take care of them both. One day the house was raided. I was nine years old then. The police burst through the door before I had left for school. The maid had planted all sorts of drugs, and firearms were found. My father was arrested.

"The papers began reporting that afternoon. By the close of business that day my father had made bail but he'd also lost several huge accounts, including the new resort he was going to build in Queenstown. Over the next few months my mother stopped being invited to her social engagements, and talk continued about my father being a drug lord. That's when Mom became sick."

Noelle had been holding her breath, her heart breaking a little more with each word he spoke. He'd only been a boy and yet he endured all this, he'd known all this was going on around him. How utterly sad.

He stood, walked to the window and slipped his hands into his pockets. "The bad dreams came first. There was always someone coming to kill her, to kill me and Dad. She rarely slept through the night, and then during the day she was so paranoid she couldn't rest. She became so jumpy I used to have to carry pockets full of change to make noise whenever I entered the room. She started talking to herself and keeping me locked in my room."

"Oh, Brock," she whispered, and came to stand behind him.

"The morning of my tenth birthday Dad said we were having a big dinner celebration. He gave Celia, the maid, the complete list of everything I wanted. Barbeque chicken, mac and cheese, biscuits, a chocolate cake and lots and lots of balloons. I loved balloons when I was younger." He smiled with the memory.

Noelle didn't hesitate but slid her arms around his waist, resting her head against his back.

"It was the last day of school and my birthday. I couldn't wait to get home. But when I arrived it wasn't to the celebration I'd been expecting. My father was being wheeled out of the house on a stretcher. I saw the blood covering his face and tried to run to him. Celia grabbed me. She held me back. In some strange way I think she wanted to protect me even though she was hired to plant evidence to destroy my father.

"The ambulance pulled off and I broke free of Celia,

running into the house to find my mother, but I couldn't find her. For two days I couldn't find her. But when the man, my father's lawyer, came to tell me that Dad was dead, Mom came out. She'd been hiding in the closet. She said they'd come to kill them so she'd gotten her gun. She'd tried to protect her husband from the killers and now he was dead." Brock took a deep breath and exhaled it roughly. "My mother killed my father."

Tears streamed down Noelle's face as she continued to hold him. He was so tense, so stiff as he spoke. She knew he was holding it in, just as the boy who had watched his parents fall apart had done. But she couldn't contain the well of hurt, the fear he must have felt and the hatred of the families who stood by and let this happen to him.

"I'm very sorry that happened to you, Brock," she whispered.

"I didn't tell you this to solicit your pity," he said, moving out of her reach.

She stumbled a bit then lifted her hands to wipe her face. "Good because I don't give pity freely. It's a waste of time." Noelle tried to sound flippant but was feeling anything but. For as mouthy and carefree as she appeared, Brock was the total opposite. He was close-lipped and resigned to his fate. He was sad but proud. She did pity him just a bit because he was too blinded by his own pain to let anyone help him.

"That's one thing we agree on. I don't like to waste time."

"Is that why you keep to yourself? Building relationships takes too much of your time?"

Brock turned to face her, then slipped his hands

into his pockets again. This must have been what he thought was a casual move. To Noelle, it was pure defensiveness. She knew because she employed it herself on occasion.

"I build the relationships that are necessary."

"Oh. Like business relationships."

"That's correct."

"But what about your personal life?"

He looked as if he were thinking about that answer for a moment. "The Donovans have been good in that regard."

"I meant a woman, Brock. What do you feel when you're with a woman?" She shouldn't have been asking that—she knew it was none of her business. But she was curious about Brock Remington, had been since stepping foot into his house. Sleeping with him had only piqued that curiosity, even though up until now she'd made a concerted effort to keep it limited to business.

He gave a half smile. "That's a weird question. Do you want to know what I feel when I'm with you, Noelle?"

"No," she answered quickly, lifting a hand to brush her hair back, although it didn't need it. "That's not what I mean. I'm asking you if you think of any woman on a long-term basis."

"No. I'm not capable of that," he stated, and meant every word.

"You're not capable of falling in love?" She noted he hadn't said that exactly, but that's probably what he meant. That bothered her on some level she surely didn't want to probe at the moment.

"I choose not to put myself in that position."

For once she wanted a real answer from him, not these clipped, frosted responses. Unfortunately for him he had no idea who he was dealing with—persistence should have been her middle name. "Why?"

He took a deep breath, then shrugged. "My parents were in love and look how that ended up. I'm a realistic man so I've got to accept that a part of them lives in me. If I put myself in a serious relationship with feelings and commitments the way they did, I'm liable to end up as hurt as my mother is today or more likely to be the one dishing out the hurt. None of that appeals to me."

With a tilt of her head and a better understanding of the man standing before her, Noelle took a step closer. "Then I will offer you my pity, whether you accept it or not. Because if you're using your parents' tragedy as your shield from the real world with real relationships, then you definitely need it."

There was no need for him to respond. She'd given him a look of sheer hopelessness before leaving him alone. Once again, alone.

Brock moved to the recliner in the far corner of the room, the one piece of furniture that had belonged to his father that he'd kept. Sitting heavily in the worn leather chair, he let her words play over and over in his mind.

Could she be right? Could this have been his crutch all these years? Of course it could. He'd had that thought a million times himself. But it had been much easier to lean on the crutch rather than try the unknown.

Now, with the arrival of Noelle and her pretty smile and perky attitude, he was rethinking that position entirely.

Chapter 13

"He asked me out, on a date I mean," Noelle told Karena over the phone on Saturday afternoon.

It had been two days since the conversation in his study, two days since his birthday, and they'd managed to awake that next morning and fall right back into step, with business, that is. Funny how they could do that, both of them, put the personal in a box and keep it there until it suited them.

However, it seemed this morning Brock had wanted to take that personal right out of its box. In no uncertain terms after they'd finished breakfast and he'd informed her that he would be golfing with Kent for most of the day, he'd asked her out.

"I don't want to discuss business, Jade and Linc or any of the other family members. I want dinner with you and me, a man and a woman getting to know each other. Can you do that?" he'd said in that matter-of-fact way that she'd become accustomed to hearing from him.

For the first time in her life Noelle had been left momentarily speechless. That moment had quickly passed as she'd blinked and answered, "You say that with such authority. As if you expect me to fall right in line."

He'd smiled down at her. "I would never be fool enough to expect anything where you're concerned. You, Noelle Vincent, are clearly the unexpected."

"Well, in that case…"

He'd grabbed her hands, bringing both of them to his lips. "Don't say no. I want to spend this evening with you."

Noelle hadn't known what to do with herself, so she'd simply agreed then attempted to leave the room as quickly as possible.

Only to have him stop her.

"Don't run from me," he said in a gruff voice. His hand held her by the elbow, and he quickly maneuvered her until she was flush against his chest.

"Running isn't the answer, for either of us."

"I'm not running from you," she'd defended, but knew it was a lie.

"We've both been running and it stops now."

His mouth lowered, landed on hers in slow procession, his closed lips settling over hers as his hands slipped around her waist.

Noelle could feel his control. His entire body was tense, his touch deliberately slow, measured. Slower than they had ever touched before.

"Kiss me back," he commanded as his palms splayed over her back.

Her eyes fluttered then closed, and she'd fallen, into his embrace, into his kiss once more.

Now, she had a headache. This man stirred up the most controversial feelings in her. One minute she was straight on her path to avoid frivolous relationships, and the next…

Hadn't she told him what she wanted from a man and hadn't he then told her the other night what he wasn't capable of offering a woman? They were obviously at opposite sides of the spectrum. So why was she still so drawn to him?

"So go to dinner with him," Karena said offhand-edly. "I don't see the problem—you're practically living with him."

"I'm staying here like I would stay at a hotel, Karena. I'm not *living* with him. Besides, all our dinners up until now have been business. Everything—besides that morning we both lost control—has been business."

"That morning and his birthday. Didn't you say he opened up to you?"

"I did," Noelle admitted, wondering why she continually told Karena everything only to have it thrown back in her face.

"Then maybe he's trying to do so again."

"But why? We don't want the same things. I mean, the only thing between us is this physical pull."

"Then that's a damn strong physical pull considering you've already acted on it. Usually, it's the sexual tension that eats away at you regardless of how different you seem. But you and Brock have already gotten that out of the way. So I'm inclined to believe there's something else going on."

"No. There's definitely nothing else going on. I want

one thing and he's determined to have another. I can't start over with a man like that."

"Then why not just have fun with him while you're there?"

"You know why I can't do that. I've been just having fun all my life. It's time I settled down and acted more responsibly."

"Is that you or Jade speaking?"

"Karena, you are not helping!"

"Why? Because I'm not saying what you want to hear?"

"No," Noelle whimpered. "Because you're not trying to warn me against making another mistake."

"That's because I don't think you're making a mistake. By going out with him, I mean. From what I hear when you talk about him, you're really feeling him. Despite your differences, you are really into this man. Now, it's unfortunate that you would meet him on the heels of your latest relationship downfall, but, Noelle, you are a woman who, when she falls, she gets right back up again. So stop sitting on your butt, looking for excuses and go to dinner with the man. Damn!"

Noelle pulled the phone away from her ear, stared at it strangely, then put it back. "Are you all right, Karena? Do you need a man in your life for a night or two?"

"Ha. Ha. Very funny. No, I do not need a man… Well, okay maybe I do. But that's not where all this is coming from. Since you've decided to get your act together you've been rattling and indecisive and I don't like it. I want the old Noelle back, the one who made decisions at the drop of a dime, who was proactive and exciting."

"I'm not proactive and exciting anymore?"

"No, you're scared and cautious and downright irritating."

Noelle rubbed her forehead. "Wait a minute, I thought we were friends. You're talking as if you can barely stand me."

On the other line Karena laughed. "Nonsense. I'm talking like this because I love you and I want what's best for you. Changing the person you are is not the answer to your love-life problems—it's making better choices. And Brock Remington seems to be a much better choice than Luther Simmons."

"I hear you," Noelle acquiesced. "I do. I'm just not so sure right now and until I'm positive…"

"You're going to starve until you're positive?" Karena asked.

"No." Giving in to her own laughter, Noelle could only appreciate Karena's honesty. "I'm going to have dinner with Brock, but I'm not, under any circumstances, sleeping with him again."

"Honey, I'm not the one you need to make that pledge to."

She'd hung up with Karena and dressed in casual linen capris and her favorite powder-blue tank top. On her feet she slipped on white wedge-heel Prada sandals and headed downstairs.

Brock's house was on seventy-five acres of land that after four weeks she'd yet to see. So since it appeared she had the afternoon to herself, and a ton of stuff on her mind, Noelle set out to do just that.

She passed the pool, in which she'd enjoyed at least a swim a day. It was great to have this weather and this scenery as she swam, and she loved the privacy. Moving beyond the pool, she stepped off the stone pathway into cool grass. A landscaper was out once a week to tend to the land when Brock was too busy to do it himself.

If she went to the left, she'd be heading toward the garage and the dirt path that led out toward the road. Instead she turned right, sighing as the gorgeously green grass opened up to scattered trees and patches of flowers that gave off a contented feeling that Noelle had secretly longed for.

Walking, she let her mind go blank, reveling in the serenity of the moment, only to have it interrupted by the impending date with Brock.

She'd agreed to go so there was no backing out now—that wasn't the type of woman she was. She'd go and she'd do everything in her power to keep it as casual as she could. Although the light in Brock's eyes this morning said he was thinking anything but casual. That was exactly what Noelle was afraid of.

Not Brock, the man, but the implications of him being interested in her. The sex part was clear—they were extremely attracted to each other in that way so much so that they'd acted on it after knowing each other only a few hours. So why hadn't the desire subsided? Probably because it was now being compounded with something else.

For all that she thought Brock was too quiet and too focused on being alone, she found herself liking him more and more every day. For his strength and his dedication, she admired him. On more than one occasion she'd found herself wondering how it would feel to be Brock Remington's woman, to be the one to open his heart to love.

But that was too big of a task for even her and her adventurous nature to take on.

She stopped for a moment beneath a huge tree with heavy branches and pretty purple blooms. At the tree's base were bundles of hosta plants. The shade was welcome as she stood looking out toward the water. This whole scene was new and invigorating to her. *A great place to start over,* she thought, then shook her head to free the silly notion.

Taking a few long strides her shoes echoed as she stepped onto the private dock and walked along the wooden planks. On both sides she was surrounded by the Miles River. Tiny rivulets moving almost silently beneath her cast a willowing perimeter to Brock's house. Arriving at the edge of the pier, she decided to sit for a minute and bent down to unsnap her sandals and take them off.

As Noelle let her bare feet hang over the side to touch the surface of the water, she felt her cell phone vibrate in her pocket. Recognizing the chime as receipt of a text message she clicked the button to show the text and cringed.

Thinking about you. Need to talk to you soon.

Why couldn't Luther simply leave her alone? It couldn't be that he just wanted her back. That was crazy since it seemed he had more than enough lovers. Their breakup hadn't been emotional or turbulent like some she'd had before. He should have simply walked away and yet he hadn't. And like a fool, she'd continued to take his calls and texts without complaint, without reporting him to the authorities for harassment.

But Noelle knew the reason for that. She didn't want

anyone to know how stupid she'd been. How vulnerable and naive she'd allowed herself to be over this man.

Turning off her phone, she dropped it onto the wooden planks beside her and tried to take deep breaths. Maybe by the time she returned to Vegas, Luther would have moved on to the next flavor of the month and decided to leave her alone.

That was a big maybe, she admitted.

She wasn't returning his calls.

Luther Simmons took one final puff on his cigarette, then tossed it into the gutter as he walked down The Strip.

He hadn't seen her at the Gramercy in weeks—that alone had concerned him. Then the mysterious phone call from Claudette yesterday, saying she had something to discuss about his latest indiscretion assured him that something wasn't right.

Not that he'd needed Claudette to confirm that fact. Ever since losing Noelle, Luther's life had gone steadily to hell.

His last two real estate deals had fallen through, the properties going to lower bidders, and his own mortgage was two months past due thanks to all his losses at the blackjack table.

Now his wife was on his back about receiving her monthly allotment and threatening him with divorce. There were times when Luther actually considered calling her bluff on that one. But then he'd think that it was cheaper to keep her since he had no doubt that Claudette would do everything in her power to leave him penniless.

And that was a situation that Luther Simmons refused to live through again. He'd grown up in the projects of Detroit, sharing a room with his four brothers and two sisters. No, never again, he'd told himself the moment he'd stepped off the plane after serving his four years in the Army. Every check the government had paid him Luther invested into Las Vegas properties, knowing that the casinos were where the money was. He'd moved to Vegas then and hadn't looked back since.

Now all of that was in jeopardy, and it was partly his fault.

He'd known there was something special about Noelle Vincent the day he met her. And when she'd walked out of his life Luther thought he'd be okay without her. He'd simply do what he always did, regroup and replan.

Claudette's interference had now changed his course of action.

Stopping, Luther adjusted his sunshades on his eyes and tilted his head back to stare at the building in front of him.

The Gramercy Casino. This was where it had all begun for him. His previous plan for success, that is. Claudette had only wanted him for the money he could give her—she didn't love him. Noelle, however, was young and impressionable. In her gorgeous hazel eyes he'd seen a naïveté that almost called to him. With Noelle he could afford to leave Claudette. Noelle had money, or rather, she was closely related to money. Donovan money.

The wheels of Luther's mind began to click. Yes, this was where it had all begun. How befitting that the Gramercy II would be where it all culminated.

Chapter 14

The evening had cooled down significantly so that there was a slight breeze. It was warm until they came closer to the water.

Brock walked beside her, holding her hand in his. To anyone passing by they probably looked like lovers, but Noelle knew differently.

Or at least she thought she did. Once again the conflict that Brock Remington set in motion in her body and her mind was evident. After speaking to Karena earlier today she'd had even more time to contemplate this evening and what it could possibly mean to their relationship. Brock said it wasn't about work, which meant it could only be about them.

He wanted to get to know her better? *Why?* she thought dismally. She'd be out of his life in two more months. Looking around at the small streets and restaurants just coming alight with the evening crowd, she let herself ponder that for a moment. She'd never been to the east coast before, never even thought about traveling here. But she'd been here almost four weeks now and was beginning to feel like she could come back, to this small town and its friendly citizens and beautiful scenery. She could take a vacation here, stay in one of the many bed-and-breakfasts, be pampered and enjoy herself. She could do that.

But not right now. Now was for business, which meant that this dinner with Brock was a bad idea. But then she'd already thought that.

Noelle absolutely hated this. It was a side of herself she didn't see often, ever actually. Questioning herself, doubting her reasoning, wanting to draw back and not deal with circumstances in her life just wasn't her thing. Well, okay, the not dealing with the circumstances of her life might be more of the Noelle that Jade had always known and that Trent had picked up on. But that's the part she'd tried to change. Whoever said growing up was easy lied big-time.

"I picked a seafood and steak restaurant. I hope that's okay with you," Brock said.

"Hmm? Oh, seafood. That sounds good," she said, trying to get her mind back on the here and now. She was out to dinner with him so there was no going back on that now.

When he stopped walking and turned to stand in front of her, Noelle felt a jolt. He smelled terrific and looked even better. Tonight he'd chucked his jeans and wore black slacks instead. His Timberland boots had been exchanged for Christian Dior moccasins—yep, she'd spied them the moment he walked into the living room where she'd been waiting for him. Her love of shoes didn't stop at women's styles, and this was a good choice for Brock. His normally rugged handsomeness had been transformed to a subtle sexiness in his dark pants and crisp white fitted polo shirt. The black sports jacket he slipped on just before escorting her out the door only topped his ensemble off and sent shivers of desire down Noelle's spine.

So it was no wonder she couldn't keep her eyes off him. Lifting her head just slightly, her gaze met his.

"I want you to remember that tonight is about you and me. Not the casino."

She opened her mouth to say something and he put a finger up, held it just a whisper away from her glossed lips until she snapped them shut.

"It's about us."

The smile came easily because he looked so good and sounded so sincere. Knowing that this was probably another mistake, but that it was too late to turn back now, she nodded her agreement.

Once inside Noelle let her attention drift to the ambiance of the restaurant Brock had chosen for them. The St. Michaels Crab and Steak House was a casual restaurant, its menu apparent by the ship paraphernalia hanging tastefully on the walls. It was a little after seven and seemed like prime time for the dinner crowd because Noelle didn't see one empty table available.

When the host greeted them Brock only gave his name and the young girl's smile spread quickly. Apparently she wasn't the only one that thought he looked good, Noelle surmised.

"Right this way, Mr. Remington. Your table is all ready."

So he'd made reservations—that meant he'd given this evening some thought. Noelle squelched a bubble of excitement at that thought. No way was Brock Remington interested in her in that way. He was simply trying to sleep with her again. *Wasn't he?*

Noelle thought that overall she was a pretty good judge of character so this would be an elaborate setup on Brock's behalf if it were just about sex. That didn't mean it was along the lines of what Noelle wanted out of a relationship, either. Hadn't he already told her he had nothing to offer a woman long term?

"So what would you like?" Brock asked when they'd sat down at the table. He'd already opened his menu and was studying it as if he'd never seen it before.

With a shake of her head, Noelle tried to stop over-analyzing every little thing. As Karena had said, she needed to stop being so indecisive. Brock Remington was a good man, of that she was fairly certain. Was he the man for her? Well, the jury was still out on that one.

"I think I'll have the stuffed shrimp," she said after a glance at the menu, which she then folded and set down on the table. Sitting back in the chair, Noelle took a deep, cleansing breath.

"That sounds good. I'm going to have the steak. And afterward we'll have some big juicy Maryland blue crabs."

After their orders were taken and glasses of wine placed in front of both of them, Brock looked at her once more. He had a habit of doing that, just looking at her. She was almost positive he liked what he saw but his gaze said there was more. *How much more?* she thought, and felt the waves of hope building.

"Tell me about your life back in Vegas," he said, leaning back in his chair, as well.

"Why?" she asked before she could help herself.

"Because I want to know all about Noelle Vincent."

That, Noelle thought, was a very real statement on his part. She believed he wanted to know about her but still wondered why.

"I live with Linc and Jade. I work at the casino," she told him.

"And what do you do for fun?"

Noelle chuckled. "Well, if you ask Linc and Jade, they'll say everything I do is for fun. Shopping for shoes, swimming for hours, getting my hair and nails done."

"I'm not asking Linc and Jade."

She tilted her head as she gazed at him. "No, you're not. I like to shop for shoes and get my hair and nails done. Jade has a wonderful day spa that I spend a lot of time at. I also enjoy swimming."

He nodded slightly. "So I've noticed. I don't think my pool has been used more since I first moved in."

"Sorry. It's therapeutic."

As if her words were spoken in another language he blinked quickly then asked, "Really? How? And what would you need therapy for?"

Noelle cleared her throat. "It's just how I unwind, how I keep myself focused on the things I need to do."

"Things like work?"

"Like work and choices I need to make. I just find that while I'm swimming my mind is totally at ease. I can think more clearly and really understand what I need."

"And that would be what, Noelle? What do you need?"

Oh, man, was that a loaded question. If she were the old throw-caution-to-the-wind Noelle she would probably say she needed him hot, hard and ready between her legs. But now that she'd matured and decided on another course for her personal life she had to contemplate the answer a little more because the first answer was still very true but even more dangerous.

Just then their food arrived and she was saved. "Right now I need to eat," she said cheerfully, and quickly picked up her napkin and eating utensils.

"Lesson number one," Brock said, putting his plastic bib around his neck and tying it. "Never underestimate how messy eating crabs can be."

"You look ridiculous in that thing." Noelle chuckled.

"Laugh if you want but I've got a feeling you're not going to be in such a good mood when you drop seasonings and bits of meat on that pretty white dress you're wearing."

Noelle looked down at her clothes and nodded. "Say no more." She was tying the plastic bib around her neck and dropping an extra napkin in her lap. When she looked up again it was to find him staring at her.

"You look—" he began.

"Ridiculous. I know." She caught herself finishing the sentence for him.

"No. I was going to say adorable."

They'd been doing good so far, keeping the conversation personal but light. Now his eyes had darkened a bit, his voice lowering a timbre. She liked it, liked the effect she seemed to have on him at times. Call it female empowerment or whatever, it felt good and for tonight Noelle finally decided to enjoy it.

"Thank you."

"You're welcome," he responded quickly. "Now, for lesson number two. Select a crab." Reaching onto the platter in front of them, he picked up a large crab.

They looked huge and a bit dangerous, but they smelled absolutely delicious so Noelle couldn't wait to dig in. After selecting her own crab and placing it in front of her, she waited for Brock to continue with his instructions.

"Okay, now some people use a knife to work their way through the crabs. That just gets in my way. But if you want to, here's one." He pushed a knife toward her.

Noelle shook her head. "Nope. I want to do this like the natives do."

"Good girl." He smiled, then looked down at his crab again. "Now, turn the crab over so you can see its belly."

She mimicked his movements.

"Then you remove the legs like this."

Noelle watched him, then did what he said.

"Now, the legs have meat in them, not as much as the claws or the body, but they have some. Me, personally, I don't have the patience to work that small amount of meat out of them, but the juice from them is heavenly." He put one of the small spindly legs into his mouth and sucked.

With a shrug she did the same thing, sucking until drops of seasoned juice touched her tongue. "Mmm," she said, then put that one down and quickly picked up another one.

Suddenly the taste of crabs was not all that Brock craved. To be truthful it wasn't suddenly. He'd been thinking of touching her all night, since he'd seen her standing in the living room waiting for him. The dress she wore was off her shoulders, leaving what seemed like miles and miles of creamy skin available for his perusal. As they'd sat across from each other, sharing small talk and their meal, he'd watched her pulse beat at the base of her neck and wanted to stroke his tongue there. When she laughed her head tilted, offering her long neck, and he wanted to nibble there.

Now she was sucking on those crab legs. Her lips, long since having lost the gloss of her lipstick during the meal, still looked enticing as they closed around the crustacean. He was envious at that moment, green with jealously that could possibly eat him alive if he didn't do something quickly. So without further thought Brock picked up one of his remaining crab legs and extended it to her.

She hesitated only momentarily before leaning forward, slowly lowering her lips over his offering. She sucked, her eyes on his. Her lips pulled back, then surprised him by coming back for another taste, this time her tongue gently grazed his finger. Brock's body hardened faster than a running bull. His erection was thick and hot against his leg as he continued to watch her, knowing she was feeling the same erotic spikes as he was.

What was she doing?

The question reverberated through Noelle's mind a second too late. Her tongue had already touched his skin, her body already heating in response.

She pulled away slowly and cleared her throat. "What's the next step?"

Brock took his time responding, not all that certain that his voice would come out clearly. "You split the belly open like this." Catching the long underbelly flap of the female crab, he pulled it apart and waited while she did the same. "Clean all of this off then break it in half. The treasure's inside," he said, no longer looking down at his crab but up at her.

She licked her lips nervously as she did what he said. Once she had her crab opened Noelle scooped out the meat and put it slowly into her mouth.

Brock kept his eyes on her, watching as she chewed then swallowed. "So what do you think?" he asked as his brow began to sweat.

"Delicious," was her reply.

Closing his eyes Brock cursed silently, then went about eating his crab.

"Is something wrong?" she asked when he'd finished the first one before her and reached for another.

"No. No problem," he answered quickly, and cracked open another crab. "We just need to hurry up."

Noelle didn't bother to ask why. In the span of ten minutes the air had grown thick with sexual tension. They had danced around it all evening and she figured it would finally come to a head. Still, she hadn't decided how she was going to deal with it.

Her thoughts were interrupted when Brock's hand wrapped around her wrist. "Stop it," he said in a coarse voice.

"Stop what?"

"Stop sitting there, thinking of us making love again. I'll never make it through the rest of these crabs if you don't and I'd really hate to spoil your first time."

She was already shaking her head. "I—"

"Don't do that, either. Don't lie about what's between us. It's futile and it's not going to stop the inevitable."

"Which is?"

"Come hell or high water, I'm going to make long, slow love to you tonight and you're going to enjoy every blessed moment of it."

Noelle swallowed, her heart hammering in her chest. "I can't finish eating with you holding my arm."

Her fingers were a mess with crab seasoning but before he let her go he lifted them to his mouth, taking one at a time inside to rub against the warmth of his tongue. One by one he cleaned each finger, watching her as his eyes grew darker and heavier with desire.

In that moment all was lost, her indecision, her fear of making another mistake, her business-only attitude, everything, except Brock.

Chapter 15

The second they were in his truck Brock reached for her, pulling her so that her body was half in the passenger seat and half over the console that separated them.

His lips crashed over hers in an unyielding fashion. She gasped and he cursed himself, forcing his body to slow down. "Kiss me back, Noelle," he murmured.

On a ragged moan she did just that. Wrapping her arms around his neck and tilting her head she opened her mouth to his assault. It wasn't a sweet connection, yet it wasn't the fevered exchange they'd shared in the pool, either. Brock was intent on making their next experience more memorable than the desperate act they'd shared before.

His hands moved up and down her back, cupping her bottom until she was lifted up off the seat.

"Brock," she moaned.

His kisses trailed from her mouth to her jaw to her earlobe. Her hands cupped the back of his head, guiding him, holding him.

"So soft," he moaned when his lips finally found the line of her neck that he'd been eyeing all night. "So damned soft."

Noelle's mind was a blur. The gentleness with which his lips were touching her warred with the rough grasp his hands had on her bottom. He tried to pull her closer and she tried to climb over the console. But this was a big truck, with big furnishings that probably weren't suited to the teenager-like necking she and Brock were currently engrossed in.

So with resolve that she had no idea she possessed she tried to pull out of his embrace.

"No. I'm not letting you go," he said, and Noelle froze. Then as if coming to her senses she resumed trying to dislodge herself from his grasp. For a moment she'd taken his words a little too seriously. This, again, was just sex.

"We're parked on a public street in your truck. This has got to be indecent," she pleaded.

Brock pulled back, reluctantly, and Noelle situated herself in the passenger seat, trying like hell to steady her breathing.

Dragging a hand down his face, Brock said, "Sorry about that."

"No. Don't apologize. It was my fault as much as yours."

"It's nobody's fault. Just like I said before. It's inevitable."

A fact that Noelle was sadly beginning to admit to herself.

Twenty-five minutes later they were back at the house. Noelle had already taken a seat in the living room, crossing her long legs. Brock watched, the heated waves of arousal clouding his mind, as one foot clad in the sexiest gunmetal-gray sandal he'd ever seen called to him. He'd commented on her shoes earlier in the evening only to be told that they were Manolo Blahniks shoes. The heel was at least four inches high, with a thin slash of gray stretching over her toes and two rows of what looked like chains at the ankles. The color was a direct match to the wide leather belt she wore at her waist. The off-the-shoulder white dress was just tight enough across the bodice and flaring enough from the waist down to drive him absolutely crazy.

They hadn't spoken of his confession to her the night before last, but it had been on his mind. It had done him good to get the things he'd said to her off his chest. For years they'd plagued him, and, while he'd known it was foolish to hold a grudge against his mother, he'd never been quite able to get past the anger to move forward with his life. Not until Noelle.

There was something about this woman that made him want to change, to learn, maybe, how to love. That had never been on his mind before because to love meant to be hurt or to be put in a position to hurt someone else and that's the last thing he would ever put someone through. But Noelle, in her brash and candid way, had simply told him he was being foolish, that the only thing stopping him from loving someone was him.

He was beginning to think that maybe she was right,

and if she was, then maybe she was the woman to show him how to love.

Brock sat on the couch beside her, foregoing the corny move of pretending to yawn to get his arm around her and simply pulling her up close to him.

She slipped willingly into his arms. For a moment he stared into her eyes, wondering when it was exactly that she'd crept into his heart.

When his lips touched hers it was soft and sweet. When her arms wrapped around his neck pulling him closer, the kiss deepened, grew hotter.

His hands were all over her. Saying he couldn't get enough was definitely an understatement. She moaned when he lifted one of her legs to cross his own, and when his fingers snaked up her inner thigh the soft whimper that escaped her mouth had his erection pressing painfully against the zipper of his pants.

Thank the heavens for skirts, he thought as the material simply fell away, leaving her bare parted legs for him to peruse. And the creator of thongs should receive some sort of award, maybe even a Nobel prize, Brock thought the moment his fingers found the thin slip of material and pushed it aside.

She was plump and soft and wet as hell. His finger shook momentarily as it moved through the damp folds. His body heat traveled until it touched every nuance, until his mind was so full of her his body had no choice but to complain.

For Noelle the last couple of hours had been decisive, she thought. Brock was a good man. He was polite and handsome and fun to be around. Above all that he was human, with the frailties of family problems just like her or anyone else. He hurt for the situation with his parents. He looked for a place that he could be himself, accepted, family. The Donovans had given him that, but she sensed he accepted it begrudgingly. She wanted so badly for him to know that if the Donovans accepted and loved him, then he couldn't have found a better place.

She wanted him to realize that there was love in the world. There were couples who worked out without the unfortunate circumstances that had befallen his parents. She just wanted him.

That pill had been hard to swallow, but then again, she'd known it the moment he kissed her against her bedroom door. For as much as she'd made mistakes in the past, something in the way he'd touched her that very first time had her thinking that this man was unlike the others in her life.

And so it was with those positive thoughts that she'd allowed him to kiss her. Who was she kidding? The moment he'd pulled her into his embrace she'd been lost. Truth be told she'd been well on her way to straddling him in that truck and riding him until they were both blinded with ecstasy.

But now they were here, in his house, alone. He was touching her. Oh, God, she loved his hands. One had his fingers buried in her hair, his blunt nails scraping her scalp as he pulled gently, but possessively. The other hand was touching her intimately, stroking her tender nub until she was shaking, ready for release.

"You are so damned beautiful. So desirable," he groaned, stroking his tongue over her earlobe.

In the distance, beyond the sound of their heavy breathing and moaning, Noelle thought she heard a bell.

"Looks can be deceiving," she said, then lifted her hips to better receive his thrusting fingers.

"No, you definitely look good."

He inhaled deeply. "You smell good."

He kissed the line of her neck, then extended his tongue and traced a long, hot trail down to her shoulder. "Mmm, and you taste good."

His thrusts deepened and Noelle could feel her thighs shaking. She was close, so damned close. And yet, there was that bell again, followed by his words.

"But that's not all there is to me."

"That's all I need," he murmured, then attempted to cover her mouth with his.

"No. Stop!" she all but yelled. It wasn't a bell she heard this time but a loud-ass chime, a warning signal stopping her again. With that knowledge Noelle moved and squirmed until he was no longer touching her. Adjusting her clothes she could only stare at him in disbelief. Hadn't she just convinced herself that she was doing the right thing this time? That Brock was a good guy? *If that were true how could he say what he'd just said?*

"Why?"

"I don't want this. Not like this," she shot back, feeling her nerves swishing inside. She wanted him to touch her, oh God, she did. But she wanted more than anything to be sure, to be right, this time. From what he'd said to her about not being able to give a woman any future and now about her looks being all he needed wasn't right to her.

"Noelle, I don't understand. We're consenting adults, we're attracted to each other. Why can't we act on what's between us? Is there someone else?"

"No!" she all but screamed. "What kind of woman do you think I am? If I was involved with somebody, you can bet your shiny new truck I wouldn't have hopped in the bed with you so fast.

"This is about me, Brock. So, yeah, I guess you could say there's somebody else. Not another man, just me. For years I've been with men who only saw the outside of me, who were attracted to the physical, and when they grew tired of it, they kept walking. Well, I'm tired of that. I've changed and I'm ready for my relationships to change, as well. So this time around I'm putting me first just as I expect the next man I become involved with to do." Because she was speaking the absolute truth on this subject for the first time to a man, Noelle's heart was racing. She wanted him to understand exactly what she was saying, wanted him to know that there was no gray area here. So she'd stood and was now pacing the living room. He'd remained seated but was following her movements with his dark eyes.

He looked so good and so serious sitting there with his elbows resting on his knees, his hands clasped. "If that's the way your past relationships went down, you weren't dealing with men and that was your first mistake."

She gave a shrill chuckle. "Oh, I've made plenty of mistakes, Brock. You don't even have to sit there and count them for me. I know where I've been, but now it's time to think about where I'm going." She stopped in front of him and inhaled. With a voice as steady as she could manage she finished with, "And it's not to bed with you again."

He didn't blink, he didn't stand up and puff his chest out like a man with a bruised ego. He only stared at her. "You make that sound so final."

Now she was the one clasping her hands. Then she thought that made her look foolish so she pulled her hands apart and stopped moving. "It is."

Brock nodded. "I'm not a man that's easily put off, Noelle."

"That's good to know because I'm not a woman that's easily taken on, not anymore. So if you really think there's something between us, something more than the hot sex we had a few weeks ago, then I suggest you figure out how to convince me."

She was out of the room before he could reply. Running again. She did that a lot. Whenever they had a heated discussion or a discussion that made her uncomfortable she bolted.

Normally that would bother him, but tonight it was probably for the best. A good gambler never revealed his hand too soon. And with Noelle, Brock thought pensively, one would have to be the best gambler to win.

Walking over to the window and looking out at the dark sky, the tall trees and the spreading acreage around his house, Brock began to think.

He'd thought he'd known what he wanted for his life and from a woman. Then Noelle appeared and all those thoughts shifted. Now, she'd told him what she wanted. And he understood. One too many of those bums Linc had mentioned had hurt her and now he was left to pick up the pieces. Could he rise to the challenge and did he really want to?

More importantly, was she worth what he would have to sacrifice to get it?

The answer to each of those questions was even clearer than Brock would have ever imagined. So, yes, he'd let her stew tonight, but tomorrow they'd both be dealt a different hand. And as with poker and blackjack, Noelle would either have to play or fold. Brock Remington didn't lose often, if ever, and he wasn't about to start now.

Chapter 16

Heading back to his bedroom from getting the late-night snack designed to take his mind off this unquenched desire for Noelle, Brock paused when he heard her voice. It was well after midnight and hours had passed since she'd left him in the living room alone. He'd just assumed that by now she would be asleep. Obviously not.

Her door was ajar and he stood just outside of it, listening. Yes, it was rude, but her tone hadn't seemed leisurely and it was late. He wondered who she was talking to since it was obvious she had to be on the phone with someone. Brock prayed it wasn't a man.

"Luther, it's past time for the games to stop. I'm sure your wife won't appreciate you calling me."

So, that was another one of Brock's prayers that had

gone unanswered. She was talking to a man, a married one at that. With a frown he turned to leave but was stopped by her gasp.

"What? How did she get them?"

Something in the room fell to the floor. Peeking inside he saw that Noelle had ignored it as she was pacing back and forth with her cell phone pressed to her ear.

"This can't be happening to me. Not now. Please not now," she said. "What are you going to do? How do you plan to stop her?"

Forgetting the rude factor, Brock stepped completely into the room and stood by the dresser. He openly listened to the one-sided conversation, wondering what the hell was going on.

"No. They can't get out. Luther, this is all your fault. You take care of it or, so help me, I don't know what I'll do to you!" she yelled. "Do you hear me, Luther? You better fix this—"

Her words were cut short as she turned to see Brock leaning against the dresser. His chest was bare, but he'd had enough foresight to slip on sweatpants. Usually he slept au naturel, but since he had company in the house he'd donned the pants as a precaution. Good thing he'd been thinking ahead because he doubted he would have been willing to leave Noelle or her suspicious conversation long enough to go back to his room and make himself decent.

"I've gotta go, Luther. Just take care of it and do it fast." She clapped the phone shut and tossed it onto the bed.

"What are you doing here? It's late," she said, clasping her hands in front of her.

"I know what time it is. That's why the sound of you

yelling on the phone caught my attention. Who were you talking to?"

"Nobody," she answered quickly.

"Nobody named Luther?"

With a deep sigh, she turned away from him. A half hour ago, hell, ten minutes ago, the sight of her long legs bared beneath the thigh-length lilac silk nightie would have had him harder than bricks. Now, in the wake of the conversation and at the disturbing look of worry in her eyes, he almost ignored it…almost.

"Just someone back in Vegas." She moved toward the bed and took a seat on the end of it. "It's no big deal. I apologize if I got too loud."

She sat with her back facing him. Her shoulders were straight, rigid, and her voice, just a hint away from losing it. Just as he'd told her before, Brock was tired of the front she put on all the time. She wasn't all right and there was no use in her pretending for him.

"What did he do to you, Noelle?"

"Nothing."

Brock's teeth gritted so hard he thought his jaw would crack. "Don't lie to me. He did something to you, something you expect him to fix. Now, either you tell me willingly or I'll be on the next plane to Vegas to find this Luther and beat the answer out of him."

She turned to him then, no doubt because of the edgy tone to his voice. Brock heard it himself but wasn't surprised. He was growing angrier. Each second that she held on to her composure, held whatever this problem was to herself, pushed him closer to the brink.

"It's none of your business."

"I say it is."

"Then you're wrong. I can take care of myself and my own problems," she argued.

"I didn't say you couldn't. However, I still want to know what this Luther did to you. Who is he?"

She grabbed the pillow, then dropped it into her lap and punched her fists into its sides. Good. She was finally showing some real reaction.

"He's an old friend."

"Friends don't upset you like this. Now, I'm going to ask you one more time, Noelle, and, I swear, if you lie to me…"

"He's my ex, all right!" She yelled, jumping off the bed and attempting to push past him to get to the door.

But Brock simply extended his arm, stopping her progress by clasping his hand at her waist. "Your ex is married?"

She moved her head so that she was no longer looking at him and admitted quietly, "Yes. I was involved with a married man."

Brock was silent, but he didn't let her go. He didn't know what to say at that moment because his emotions were roiling out of control. What kind of man with a wife got involved with another woman? It was a naive question, Brock knew, still the scenario pissed him off. The fact that the man was obviously still attempting to stay connected to Noelle made it even worse.

"Go ahead and say it," she began.

"What is it you expect me to say?"

"Tell me I'm a terrible person for getting involved with a married man. Call me a home wrecker, an idiot, a sl-slut."

She stammered over the last word. Brock moved quickly so that they were now face-to-face. "I can think of a lot of words to describe you but that one—" his lips closed tightly as he reigned in his temper "—that one would never cross my mind."

"But I am. I should have known. I shouldn't have disrespected his marriage. I'm always making foolish decisions, always messing up."

Her head was moving from side to side so fast her hair, which had been pulled back, fell in heavy strands until her face was mostly covered. She whimpered, and Brock pulled her closer, cradling her in his arms.

"He's the one who's married. It's his responsibility not to disrespect his marriage."

"But I should have known better."

Her voice cracked, guilt that had been stored tightly inside threatening to break free.

"Did he tell you up front that he was married?"

"No."

"Did he wear a ring?"

"No."

"Are you a mind reader?"

She paused, tilted her head and looked up at him. "No."

"Then how the hell were you supposed to know that jerk was married? You're smarter than that, Noelle. Don't blame yourself for something that you couldn't have prevented."

She was still looking up at him when one lone tear escaped, rolling down her cheek moments before her eyes closed and she put her head down onto his chest once again.

His body stirred, but it wasn't with lust or desire— it was with compassion and something else all together. Something more intense than he'd realized before.

Chapter 17

Noelle couldn't believe what she was about to do. This was her problem and she'd vowed to handle it on her own. But here, right now, in Brock's arms, she felt so protected, so safe that the words were rolling off her tongue before she had a moment to second-guess them.

"When I found out Luther was married, I cut things off with him. Immediately. I told him I never wanted to see him again. I even thought about going to his wife to apologize but figured that would be a waste of time."

They were both sitting on her bed now, Brock's arm still protectively wrapped around her shoulders.

"How did you find out he was married?"

"I was at work one day and this woman came up to me. She looked angry so I instantly thought she'd lost some money and wanted to rant about cheating slot machines or something like that. Turns out she'd been involved with Luther, as well, and wanted to rant about cheating men instead."

"How long had you been seeing him?"

"A little over three months. We met in the casino. I never even thought to ask if he was married. And I'm not normally inclined to believe the ravings of a scorned woman, but everything she said just seemed to fall into place. She knew Luther's cell-phone number, his schedule, everything. She also knew his wife's name and number and dared me to call her. But by that time I didn't need to."

Brock seemed so serious in his questioning, like he was the law and she was a victim. He had questions and only she could provide the answers, that's how their conversation went.

"What did he say when you confronted him?"

"He didn't deny it if that's what you mean. He said the woman from the casino was jealous and that his was a marriage of convenience. He was so calm and cool, as if it was no big deal. I hated myself then. Right at that moment I've never hated myself more. Of all the things I've done in my life nothing, absolutely nothing, made me feel as low as finding out I was sleeping with another woman's husband."

Suddenly things became more clear to Brock. He and Noelle had jumped right into the physical relationship, then she'd backed off. For weeks now he'd been trying to figure out why. Now, he knew. She blamed herself for this fiasco with the married man and so probably believed that any intimate decision she made was a mistake. He could go along with the fact that their intimacy had been too soon after they'd met. But he knew her better now and she knew him. Brock knew what she wanted and wondered for a split second if he could possibly be the man to give it to her.

"So what does Luther want with you now?" he asked, leaving those other surprising thoughts alone for the moment.

"His wife—" she began, and stopped. *How could she tell this man that she'd known only a month about the most painful time in her life?* She hadn't been lying—the things she'd done with Luther would forever go down in the history of her life as the worst. Unfortunately, they were now a very prominent part of her future if she didn't do something and quickly.

"Go ahead, Noelle. You can tell me. I won't judge you," Brock offered, taking one of her hands in his and rubbing it.

She took a deep breath and figured what the hell, she'd come this far. "It seems that his wife knew about Luther's affairs all along. And because I'm so damned lucky in life and love, she had us followed. Now there are pictures of us together in I'll say a compromising position that she's threatening to take to the press if Luther doesn't pay her off."

"So Luther needs to pay her to get the pictures and she'll leave you two alone?" Brock asked skeptically.

"Luther doesn't have the type of money she's asking for. She's using the fact that I'm Jade's sister to try and tap into the Donovans for the money." She looked at him directly then. "If Luther doesn't get the money from me, she'll go to the papers and smear the Donovans right along with me. After all they've done for me this is how I repay them."

The tears came full force then. Noelle's entire body seemed to convulse with them. Never had she felt so weakened, so defeated. After all they'd done, she'd be letting Jade down again. Only now there was more to it—there were the twins and Linc and the rest of the Donovan family to consider. She wasn't in this by herself, which meant she wouldn't go down alone. It was humiliating and crushing to even think of what was about to happen.

So she wasn't thinking when Brock scooped her up in his arms. The next thing she knew she was cradled against his chest as he held her like a baby. His lips touched her forehead as he shushed her.

"We all make mistakes," he said. "Weren't you the one telling me that just a few days ago?"

"Not like this," she stammered.

"No, but mistakes come in all forms and fashions."

"I don't know how to fix it."

"You don't have to."

"Yes, I do. I can't let this touch the Donovans. Jade is so happy and she has the girls. I have to do something. I've saved some money," she said as she was trying to lift up off his lap. "I'll give her that and then I'll have to see if she'll hold off for a few months until I can get the rest."

Brock was shaking his head. "Like I said, you're a lot of things, Noelle, but stupid is not one of them. What's the first thing you know about blackmailers?"

Noelle took a deep breath and wanted to roll her eyes at him but refrained. "Pay them once and they'll never stop."

"Exactly. So we're not paying her one red cent."

"'We'?"

With a finger to her chin, Brock lifted her face to his. "We. You, me or the Donovans. None of us are giving Luther or his wife a dime."

"But—" she began, stopping as his lips lightly touched hers.

"I'll take care of it," he whispered.

"It's not your problem."

"If it involves you, it involves me," he said, then kissed her lips once more.

"Please don't tell me to stop again, Noelle. I'm not trying to push you. I just need to be close to you right now." Because if she pushed him away, if he walked out of that room, he was definitely liable to get on a plane and head straight for Vegas. There was no doubt in Brock's mind that this Luther character and his wife were trying to make a fortune off his affair with Noelle, and Brock would be damned if he let that happen.

Instead of running again, as he'd half expected her to, Noelle fell into his embrace, letting his lips move sweetly over hers.

So many thoughts flitted through Noelle's mind as he lifted her into his arms, moving his lips from her mouth to her forehead and carrying her to his room. When he lay her in the center of his bed, she felt safe. It was foolish, she knew—this was just a bed, much like the one in the room she'd been calling her own. And yet, it was different. Keeping his sweatpants on, Brock lifted the comforter and slid under, holding up one end for her to follow suit.

Wordlessly, she did. He held an arm out to her and she went to him, willingly. The safeness engulfed her like a warm blanket, and when he wrapped his other arm around her, holding her tightly against his chest she sighed, wondering how she'd come to be here. No, not in this state and not necessarily in this predicament, but in his arms. In Brock's arms.

Time seemed to drift away as her words, the conversation she'd had on the phone and the conversation they'd had earlier filtered through Brock's mind. Some idiot had threatened her. That, Brock would not tolerate. She was strong and stoic and determined to deal with the situation herself, but he'd handle it once and for all.

She'd quivered when he drew her in his arms. For just a second she'd shaken, then settled against him as if finally releasing the battle going on within herself to him. Brock wasn't arrogant enough to think that his stance against her blackmailer was going to make the issues Noelle had with the two of them getting together go away. But the fact that she was now lying in his bed, her thigh cradled warmly between his, her head resting on his chest, her breathing finally coming in steady intervals, was definitely progress.

Hours later Brock was still awake, watching as Noelle's head lay against one of his pillows. And as he was just about to give in to his own fatigue it hit him. More like touched him, a featherlight stroke over his shoulder, down his chest, circling over his heart until the warmth there was steady and intense.

Despite the distance he'd purposely kept between himself, women and serious relationships, there'd obviously been a glitch. One that Noelle and her pretty smile, intense eyes and optimistic spirit had fully exposed. There was no denying it—looking away from her and back again had the same emotions swirling quickly in the pit of his stomach.

He was in love with Noelle Vincent. And there wasn't a damn thing he could do about it.

Nor did he want to.

Chapter 18

"Mr. Donovan, you're a hard man to catch up with," Brock said, leaning back in his chair with his cell phone to his ear.

He'd waited until Noelle had gone out for her swim to make this call. She'd be against what he was doing, Brock knew that for sure. But he'd deal with her wrath later. It was time to do what the men in his family did best—get down to business.

"Hey, cousin, long time no hear from," Trent Donovan answered in his deep voice. Normally that voice was no-nonsense and ready to argue, but today it was more laid-back. Brock assumed that could be attributed to Tia.

The news of Trent's fall into the whirlwind of new love had come directly from Brock's brother, Brandon, who'd had the pleasure of meeting Tia at Jade's baby shower. At that time Brandon had also seen Tia have what could only be described as some sort of breakdown and Trent literally sweeping her off her feet and carrying her away to safety. According to Brandon it had been a sight none of the Donovan men would ever forget. And now, the infamous Trent Donovan, the last of the "Triple-Threat Donovans," was happily engaged and waiting for his gorgeous fiancée to give birth to their first child. That thought made Brock smile.

He'd been thinking more and more about family and friends and lasting connections in the last day or so, and talking to Trent was only bringing those yearnings more to the forefront.

Still, there was another matter that needed to be dealt with first.

"That's because I haven't been able to track you down," Brock answered with a smile and a genuine feeling of familial connection with the man on the other line. That, too, was something Brock hadn't felt in a long time. "Your new woman been keeping you tied down?"

Trent laughed. "Come on now, Brock. You know me better than that. I'm not one to be tied down by a woman."

In the background Brock heard guffaws and laughter and comments that quickly discredited Trent's words.

"All right, all right. I'll admit that I've been incommunicado here and there, but Tia's still trying to get in modeling gigs and I'm not about to let her travel alone."

"I hear that and don't blame you one bit. She's a gorgeous woman. I'm happy for you both."

"Thanks, man. I'm telling you I never expected to find a woman that could turn me inside out like this."

Brock nodded and gazed out the window. From his office he had a view of the bottom end of the pool. Every few minutes he'd catch a glimpse of Noelle ending one lap and beginning another. Trent's words couldn't have been more true if Brock had said them himself.

"So since I'm calling you at the office and I hear voices I'll ask if I'm interrupting anything work related."

"Of course not. Linc, Max and Adam just stopped by to see what we're going to do today. We're trying to have a men's day out since the ladies are cooped up at Adam's place doing who knows what."

"So the gang's all there." He smiled, missing that closeness of family. "Wait a minute? Where's Ben?"

"Italy," Max responded giving his younger brother's whereabouts.

"What's he doing there?"

"You know how Ben is about his work. He's building a house for some heiress in Monterey and she wants it to resemble an Italian villa. Ben's all about the details. It's a shame both of you have to miss out on this men's day. We don't get a chance to get together like this often," Max said.

Brock chuckled, knowing that a men's day out with his cousins could lead to any matter of dangerous excursions. "In that case I'll just take a minute of your time."

"Man, you're family, take as much time as you like. Is something wrong?" Trent asked.

Brock rubbed the day's growth at his chin. "I think something's brewing and I sort of want to head it off before it gets too bad."

"I see," Trent said. "Hey, quiet in the peanut gallery. Brock's got something going on," he heard him say to the fellas in the background.

"Put him on the speakerphone," Brock heard Linc say.

"Brock, I'm going to put you on speaker since we're all family here. Is that cool?"

Family. There was that word again. There had always been a one-for-all-and-all-for-one mentality to the Donovan clan. Funny how being miles away and submerged in his own pity party Brock had forgotten how good that felt.

"That's fine," he said, allowing the warmth of the connection to run its course.

After a few clicks Trent said, "Okay, what's up?" His voice echoed and Brock knew he'd hit the speaker button and that now everything he said would be heard by the men of the Donovan family, *his* family.

"It's about Noelle," Brock started.

"I told you to keep your hands off her," Linc interrupted instantly.

"Come on, Linc," Brock replied. "Have you taken a good look at her? What man in their right mind could keep his hands off her?"

Maxwell Donovan, the son of Everette and Alma Donovan, Everette being the middle brother of Henry and Albert, Brock's adoptive father, spoke up then. "I know exactly what you mean, Brock. Noelle was attractive when I first met her and Jade, but in the past couple of years I've watched her morph into a beauty men line up to get near."

"Both of you need to keep your eyes on someone else. Noelle's off-limits," Linc insisted.

"I agree," Brock stated. "She's off-limits to you, Max, and to any other man who even thinks of getting close to her." Then he took a breath and said, "Except me, of course."

There was a moment of silence on the other end, then Adam laughed. "Man, I tell you the Donovan men are falling like dominoes."

"What? Brock, you and Noelle are supposed to be doing business," Trent stated.

"We are. Some very personal business."

"I hear you, man. I definitely hear you on that," Max added.

Linc groaned, "Jade's going to kill me."

"Relax, Linc. She knows Brock is one of us. Noelle couldn't be in better hands," Trent added in Brock's defense.

"If that's the case, then what are you calling for, Brock? You can't handle the feisty Noelle on your own?"

This was from Linc, and on a normal day Brock probably would have gone right along with his ribbing and the testosterone-filled conversation about the woman in his life. But today wasn't the day. Things were too strained for that.

"She's in trouble," Brock stated solemnly.

"What kind of trouble?" Linc asked first.

"What do you know about the guy she was seeing a few months before she left Vegas? She said his name was Luther."

"Luther Simmons. Jade told me about him. He's some real estate mogul out here that she met at the casino. I found out later that he was married and Noelle dropped his ass when she found out. I didn't tell Jade that part."

"Well, apparently Luther isn't used to being dropped. He called her last night and had her so upset she was trembling."

"So he's stalking her?" This was Trent, the lethal

tone of his voice a stark contrast to the jovial tone of a few minutes ago.

"I'm thinking that's probably what he's been doing for the last few months. But last night he stepped up his game."

"Please tell me he threatened her," Trent began. "I haven't had any good action since that lunatic woman tried to come after Tia."

That was just like Trent. He'd officially retired from the Navy SEAL team he'd been with for more than ten years, but that combative edge was a permanent part of his persona.

"Not exactly. He and his wife are attempting to blackmail her."

"You've got to be kidding me," Max muttered. "Him *and* his wife? Are you serious?"

"That's what Noelle said when I made her tell me about the phone call."

Linc gave a dry chuckle. "You *made* Noelle do something? Yeah, you two must be involved, otherwise she would have cut your balls off and served them to you for dinner."

Brock had to agree. "Yeah, a couple of times it looked like she was considering doing just that. But she told me about the affair and how she ended it. She said he's been calling her a lot, and last night he made a proposition—either she pays him and his wife a half million dollars or some pictures the wife snapped of Noelle and her cheating husband will go public."

"So the idiot and the scorned wife are teaming up. That's real cute," Adam added.

"Noelle doesn't have half a million dollars. Why would they even ask her for that type of money?" Max asked.

"Because she's the manager of the Gramercy, which is owned by one of the infamous Donovans, who just happens to be married to her sister. You get the picture?" Brock stated.

"I get it loud and clear," Trent said. "Luther needs his ass kicked and his wife needs to find another way to make her money. Donovans don't take kindly to extortion."

"Donovans don't take kindly to men messing with their women," Linc added.

"Exactly," Brock piped in. "So what I need you to do, Trent, is find out who this guy is. I mean everything. I want to know how many teeth he has in his mouth, just so I can keep count when I knock them out."

"Yeah. I'll do that. And I'll find out about his wife, too," Trent replied.

"Linc, you have to keep this from Jade for as long as possible. If she finds out she's going to call Noelle and then—"

"Noelle's going to rain all over your hero parade," Linc finished. "I know. I'll keep it quiet. But you keep her safe."

"I'm not going to let anything happen to her," Brock promised, and meant each word with an intensity that was changing his mind about a lot of things.

"I figure they've given her a deadline, but she hasn't shared that with me, so sooner rather than later on the background info on this guy. We need to know exactly what he's capable of before we handle him."

"He's got his hands pretty deep in the real estate market here so he's got some cash of his own," Adam said. "But I can make some calls, see what his portfolio is looking like. I don't know much about the wife."

"They just bought a huge place over in the Palisades.

The one we were looking to buy and convert," Max, who was also Adam's business partner, added.

"Yeah, that probably put a pretty big dent in his capital."

"I'm thinking the wife might be looking for some type of financial settlement as payment for his dallying," Brock said thoughtfully.

"It's a shame. For some people it's all about the money."

Linc sighed. "Sad but true."

"Noelle and I have a cocktail party some local politicians are giving in honor of the new casino to attend tonight so I'm hoping that will get her mind off the situation for a while. Can you guys get back to me tomorrow with a status and we'll go from there?"

"Sure thing," Trent said.

"And, Brock…" This was Linc again with that warning tone in his voice.

"Yeah?" Brock answered, not sure he was going to take kindly to another warning from his cousin, as if he were the bad guy.

"I'm glad you're the one she's opening up to."

The smile that touched Brock's lips was small, but the warmth that spread throughout his chest was massive. Never had he needed approval from anyone for anything that he did. But this time, from this man, it felt good. "Thanks, cuz," he said, then disconnected the call.

The wheels were in motion now and Luther Simmons was going to be very sorry he'd ever bumped into Noelle Vincent. Brock was personally going to make sure of that.

Chapter 19

Everybody who was anybody was decked out in evening elegance in the main ballroom of the Gramercy II. For tonight's function the gaming was just for fun. It was an unofficial opening that allowed all the political figures and St. Michaels's elite citizens to peruse and get a taste of their newest attraction.

Brock walked in and for the first time wasn't disturbed by the fact that all eyes suddenly turned on him. That was most likely because those eyes weren't really on him but on the gorgeous woman that stood beside him.

She wore an orange dress that on any other woman might have looked gaudy or even ridiculous. But against Noelle's honey complexion and highlighted by her hazel eyes and exotically tinted hair it was a perfect combination. Her shoes—another pair of something designer that he couldn't remember the name of—were gold and slinky, matching the two barely there straps at her shoulders that held the dress in place. The shimmering material hugged her curves until Brock felt as if he were choking.

She was beaming and bubbling with excitement, having chatted all the way on the ride from his house to the casino about the opening and the décor and layout. She was nervous, he knew. But she hid it well. She was also weakening to him, just a little bit.

After his call to Trent late this morning, Brock had fixed lunch for him and Noelle, taking it out by the pool where she was. When she'd finished her laps, she joined him on the lounge with the table between them and they'd shared a pleasant meal together.

Brock hadn't broached the subject of their relationship again because she'd stated what she needed and he knew what he wanted. Now, he would make it happen.

As he'd told himself before he'd let his body rule his common sense, the seduction of Noelle Vincent would be slow but in the end, more than worth it.

The duration of their afternoon had consisted of fine-tuning last-minute details for tonight's party. Noelle was a perfectionist when it came to business, which suited Brock just fine.

It was good to see that all their hard work had paid off. Not only was the Gramercy II a structural beauty, but its theme and décor provided more than your normal gaming fantasy. Noelle and Josette had been absolutely right about the colors. Muted beiges, soft yellows, sage greens created a stylish seashore haven. The lights were dim, spotlighted in strategic corners in fierce golds. The waterfall in the main entrance was entranc-

ing, its sound lulling as guests moved from room to
room. Up three levels the resort rooms were even more
spectacular in a soft, understated way. The VIP sections
were in regal red, forest green and gold, whereas the
general public suites carried burgundy and gold throughout. It was a masterpiece, their masterpiece. His and
Noelle's.

The stream of well-wishers that approached Brock and
Noelle was growing thicker. Having already spoken to the
mayor and his wife and the two congressmen that had
pushed for the legalization of gaming in the state, Brock
and Noelle were all smiles for the rest of their guests.

Next up were the pillars of the community, or should
he say the wealthy socialites that would no doubt be
dropping lots of cash in the Gramercy II. For this reason
alone Brock and Noelle continued to smile, to talk and
to endure the grueling task of networking.

"Brock Remington," an older woman, whose silver-
gray hair was pulled back so tightly that her eyes slanted
drastically upward, said as she approached them, holding her hand out for Brock.

Almost mechanically, Brock took her hand, kissed its
back then proceeded to shake the man's hand beside her.
He held on to that man's hand just a bit stronger when
he noticed his eye cutting over to Noelle. More than one
man had perused her in that mouthwatering dress, and
on more than one occasion Brock had felt as if he could
actually commit murder.

"And who might this lovely young lady be?" the
woman asked.

"I'm Noelle Vincent, site manager for the Gramercy
II. And you are?"

The woman clenched a gold sequined bag. "My name is Marilyn DeSalvo and this is my husband, Enrique. We knew Brock's parents."

Noelle felt Brock stiffen the moment the woman's words were out. They'd been enjoying themselves the past hour at this party they'd had no choice but to attend, and now this. Already knowing how Brock felt about the story of his parents, she touched a hand to his elbow for reassurance.

"Have you had a chance to walk around and see the magnificent building that Brock has built?" Noelle asked Mrs. DeSalvo, whose slanted eyes held a hint of malice.

"If you've seen one casino, my dear, you've seen them all," was her blithe response.

"I beg to differ," Brock jumped in. "The Gramercy II has several different attractions, not to mention our world-class resort. There are two rooms ready tonight. If you and Mr. DeSalvo would just step over here, we'll have you set up for a tour."

Marilyn only smiled. *A slightly chilling sight,* Noelle thought.

"No, dear, that's of no interest to me. When I received this invitation, it was among so many others like it, but your name caught my eye and my memory came rushing back. Or should I say the memory of the scandal your parents created returned."

"Thank you," Brock said, standing rigidly. "I'm glad that the memory could bring you out tonight. Are you a resident of St. Michaels or just visiting?"

"We have a home here in St. Michaels and one in Cambridge. My husband plays golf with your very fine mayor here. That's how we came into the invitation. And imagine my surprise when I recalled that you were the son of Jure and Tarine Remington."

Noelle continued to rub her hand over Brock's elbow, noting that the tension now rolled off him in thick heavy waves. And she could certainly see why. This woman obviously knew of what happened with Brock's parents. It was also painfully clear that Mrs. DeSalvo's entire purpose here tonight was to let Brock know that she knew.

"Your parents would be proud, son," Enrique interrupted.

Brock cleared his throat. "Thank you."

"Yes. They certainly would be proud. Especially of this pretty young lady you've chosen."

When Brock was about to respond, Noelle cut in. "Actually, I'm the one who is proud to be with Brock this evening. He's an exceptionally talented man and it's been a pleasure working with him," she said in a voice just as deceivingly sweet as Mrs. DeSalvo's.

"Yes. Well, your name doesn't sound familiar, dear, so I can only assume that you are not from St. Michaels."

"No. I'm from Las Vegas."

"Oh, I see, the casino capital of the world."

Noelle smiled back in return. "Well, when you want to create the best, you need to start at the top."

Mrs. DeSalvo raised a brow. "I'm wondering, in your haste to create the best casino, did you bother to check out the dark past of the construction company you hired?"

"Remington Construction was selected based on their proven ability to get the job done," was Noelle's tight response. This woman was steadily getting on her nerves.

"I'm sure. I'm sure," DeSalvo said. "But what I'm

referring to is, from what type of family the owner of said company is from."

Noelle didn't miss a beat. "Fortunately, I know several of his family members and can speak highly of them all."

"Then clearly you aren't speaking about the Remingtons of Cambridge. The Jure Remington who was brutally gunned down by his wife after it was revealed that he was nothing more than a drug-smuggling fraud."

With those words Brock took a cautious step closer to Mrs. DeSalvo, whose husband was now glaring at her in annoyance. Noelle stepped with him, her hand tightening on his arm.

"Mrs. DeSalvo, unfortunately I don't believe that you and your husband are welcome here. You're invitation is now revoked. Please leave," Brock said in a tight, stern voice.

Again, Mrs. DeSalvo only smiled. "It's only right that she know everything. Especially with the way she's standing so close to you and you giving off that possessive sneer to any man who dares look twice at her. It's only fair that she know exactly what type of man she's dealing with."

"Thank you, Mrs. DeSalvo, for your consideration. I'm well aware of the type of man that Brock Remington is, just as I am aware of the fine upstanding citizen his father was before he was maliciously framed."

"Is that what he told you? In addition to knowing the Remingtons, I've also been a longtime friend of the late Mr. and Mrs. Truesdale."

Noelle looked to Brock, who said, "Truesdale was my mother's maiden name."

DeSalvo nodded. "Precisely. I was there when Tarine

brought home the less-than-deserving Jure Remington to present to her parents. I was also there when her parents told her that she was out of her mind to think they would allow her to marry the man and that he would only bring bad news to their family. And just look what happened."

Brock was already signaling for one of the security guards at the door.

"That's enough, Marilyn," Mr. DeSalvo said.

"No. It's not enough. I swore to Lillian that if I ever got the chance I would protect the next innocent woman to fall prey to the shenanigans of a Remington and that's what I intend to do."

"Then your intentions are misplaced, ma'am. Because I have no desire to turn my back on Mr. Remington based on your scandalous lies. I suggest you go back and recheck this history that you are so compelled to bring up."

The security guards had arrived.

"The DeSalvos were just leaving," Brock said.

Then one of the guards looked at Mrs. DeSalvo, who had yet to move. Her husband, with a grim face, nodded and took her by the arm, moving her in the direction of the door. Pausing momentarily, Mr. DeSalvo turned back to Noelle and Brock with a look of apology on his face but no words.

The rest of the evening was tense, to put it mildly, with Brock walking around, going through the motions and Noelle staying close just in case the inevitable breakdown occurred. But to his credit Brock survived the evening schmoozing and networking just the way he was supposed to. It wasn't until the building was finally empty and only the two of them remained that his real feelings showed.

"I thought it was behind me. I thought I had finally escaped," he said as they walked around, turning out lights. They were in one of the private gaming rooms and just about to leave.

"My Grammy used to always say that good gossip never dies," Noelle offered, trying to remain upbeat.

"I guess your Grammy was right."

"Yeah. Most of the time she was. But the thing about gossip, Brock, is that you don't have to believe it. Nobody has to believe it or even listen to it. It's a choice and people that know you will make the right choice if they should hear Mrs. DeSalvo's cruel insinuations."

"I know that. I just thought it was over. When I decided to come back to Maryland, I knew it wouldn't be to Cambridge, but I wanted to be close to the place that they loved. To the small Eastern Shore town where they'd met and fallen in love. I thought it would make me closer to them."

"That's why you kept your mother close, as well?"

He nodded. "I tried for years to visit her, on her birthday, on their wedding anniversary and on my birthday. But with each year she seemed to fade more and more until finally I couldn't see the point in continuing. She has no idea who I am or who she is."

"I don't believe that."

He turned at her words.

"I believe she knew. I just think that the memory is buried deep within her, along with all the good memories. That's what people do sometimes to protect themselves. They bury the good and hope that the bad will pass."

Pushing back his jacket, Brock slipped one hand in

his pants pocket. "Is that what you did? Did you bury the good in your life, hoping that your bad choices would disappear?"

"Sort of," she said, noting that now the conversation had turned to her.

She didn't mind. Knowing him as she did now she'd been sure that his delve into his past wasn't going to last long. He didn't know it, but he was doing exactly what she'd said, burying the good and hoping the bad would pass—only his bad wasn't going to pass until he forgave his mother.

He looked so solemn standing there. A look she hadn't seen in a couple of days. In his black tuxedo and white shirt and vest, he was GQ handsome and more desirable than she'd ever realized. But that wasn't what struck her. It was the cord of loneliness in his voice, the way the deep timbre reached out to her, touching her, summoning her to do…something, anything to make it better.

Last night Brock had been there for her. He'd calmed her through the fear and panic of Luther's threat. He'd sworn to help her and he hadn't judged her. That had been the most important part, the thing that had taken her aback yet was profoundly relieving. He'd accepted the mistake that she made but didn't hold it against her. It had taken her more than a year to forgive herself and he'd done it in just seconds.

And he hadn't stopped there. He'd held her all through the night making her feel not only safe and protected but, for once in her life, cherished. When she'd awakened this morning he'd already been up and in the office, which she'd suspected was his way of letting her out of an uncomfortable situation. Yet it wasn't uncomfortable at all. Waking in Brock's bed was more right then Noelle had ever dared to admit.

"You owe me one," she said, and watched as his brow furrowed in confusion.

"I owe you one what?"

"You won the race so I want a second shot."

The frown increased. "We're standing in the middle of a casino, Noelle. I don't really see how we're going to have a swim race right now."

"No." She shook her head and took a step closer to him. "Something else I know I'm good at."

This time he looked intrigued. "And what might that be?"

With a nod toward the table that Brock was standing closest to she smiled and said simply, "Poker. What else?"

Chapter 20

Brock had removed his tuxedo jacket and was now sitting across the green felt table from Noelle. Where she'd found a deck of cards he had no idea, but she was presently shuffling them like a pro. Of course, they were in a casino so it should have been a given where she'd found them. The question was when had she gotten them and where she'd kept them. Nothing could be hidden beneath that dress she wore, nothing but her gorgeous body.

All night long he'd been salivating as he watched her. Well, up until the point that the DeSalvos had appeared. Still, even with that nasty episode, Brock hadn't lost sight of Noelle, nor had he lost the deep hunger for her that was now threatening his sanity. Damn, it was hard trying to be a gentleman where she was concerned, especially when with each shuffle of the cards her breasts jiggled, expanding the already fine display of creamy cleavage.

"What are the stakes?" he asked, trying to keep his mind off her body and on the game at hand. Admittedly, the suggestion of a game of cards at the end of this long, tension-filled evening wasn't exactly what Brock had in mind. But as diversions went, it would be fun, as he was sure was Noelle's intention.

Noelle paused with half the deck of cards in one hand, the other half in the opposite hand. Tilting her head, the corners of her lips tipped in a smile. "Those," she said, and nodded to him.

Brock looked down at himself then back up at her. "My cufflinks?"

She shook her head.

"My watch?"

With another negative nod, Noelle pushed the cards toward him, indicating that he should cut the deck. With slow movements Brock did so, then looked up at her with a raised brow. "My shirt?"

Her smile widened, then she licked her lips seductively. "And whatever other pieces of clothing you should lose."

Well, well, well, Brock thought with heat rising steadily in his groin. This diversion just might be more than fun. "Or whatever pieces of clothing *you* should lose."

"Not a chance," she said confidently. "You had your chance at winning and you collected your prize. Now, it's my turn."

She began to deal and Brock watched her carefully. If she lost a hand he'd have her releasing those straps from her shoulders. He wanted to see her breasts, with the urgency of a man dying of thirst. Then again, if she won this hand he was betting she'd ask for his shirt first. In which case he'd tell her she needed to take it off. Then her hands would be on his bare skin. One hand fell into his lap and before he could stop it stroked his length. He was going to come out of this game a winner either way.

"Texas hold'em," she stated, drawing his attention back to the cards. "Blinds?"

Brock cleared his throat. "Hmm, the lady likes a challenge," he said, then considered his blind bet while his hand hovered over his two hole cards.

She was placing the last of the five community cards in the center of the table, then neatly stacked the remaining deck to the left.

"I want those straps," he replied.

She looked at him strangely for a moment. "With only my teeth I want to pull each strap from your shoulders, then watch the top half of that sinful dress fall."

A flicker of desire lit her eyes as her fingers ran slowly over her hole cards still facedown on the table. "I'll raise your bet. I want your shirt," she said softly. "Quick and completely I want it off and your chest bare."

Brock swallowed as she picked up her cards. He'd known that's what she'd go for first, but actually hearing her say it had his heart pounding.

She performed the flop, dealing three community cards faceup on the table. Lifting her two hole cards, she surveyed them and the three cards revealed.

Brock was now looking at his hole cards and at the community cards, trying like hell not to stare at her breasts or imagine them exposed for his perusal.

She nodded in his direction, indicating that he should begin the second round of betting.

"The dress comes off, completely. I'm going to peel it off of you just as I'd peel a sweet, juicy orange." With his bet stated, Brock took a card from the community deck.

"I'll take your belt," she said. "Have you ever been tied up, Brock?"

No, he thought, *but he was about to pass out from low blood flow.* Her words had it all dropping to his already thick erection.

Two more rounds, two more bets and Brock was ready to fold his hand and throw her up onto this table. Making love to her in the casino wasn't exactly his idea of seducing her, but he'd let that minor infraction slide for the blissful release, the inevitable pleasure of slipping into her slick heat once more.

Noelle surveyed her cards. Two nines, two threes and a six. She looked at Brock, who looked confident, devilishly handsome and just a tad dangerous. She'd noticed throughout the betting process how dark his eyes had grown, how sensual his looks at her had become.

When she'd suggested this game of poker she hadn't really thought it through. Karena would be glad to know that the impulsive Noelle was back. She'd wanted simply to take his mind off the altercation with the DeSalvos, to give him a reprieve from the trauma of his childhood.

Instead she'd succeeded in arousing them both to a point that they may not recover from. She'd pushed him away last night, giving him the rules of her own game. If he wanted her he had to work for it, to prove it wasn't just about sex. And here she was, twenty-four hours later, tempting him, tempting herself.

"Well?" his husky voice stroked the already burning fire inside her.

"Well, yourself?" she quipped. Just because she was ready to jump his bones didn't mean she had to let him know that.

With a smile that was designed to have any and all women within reach dropping their panties on command, Brock spread his cards onto the table. He waited a beat, letting her look her full at him, then down at the table.

Damn, Noelle thought as she surveyed the cards. *Hot damn!*

"A full house," she replied. "Very impressive."

Placing her cards faceup on the table, Noelle sat back in her chair, waiting for Brock's reaction to her two pair. *He'd won again,* she thought and couldn't remember if that was supposed to be a good or bad thing. All she knew right now was that one of Brock's wagers had been to peel her dress off her like peeling an orange. Her entire body shivered. Another bet had been to lick every exposed inch of her skin. Her thighs quivered.

No, she didn't give a damn who had what cards. All she was concerned about at this moment was how fast he could get around this table and get his hands on her.

"Two pair," Brock whispered. "Too bad. I win."

He was already standing, pushing his chair back so hard it fell to the floor. Noelle didn't know whether to stand or sit or possibly run. She opted to stand just a second after he reached for her, pulling her up out of the chair.

"Did you wear this dress on purpose?" Brock asked, loosening his hold on her arms until his fingers were running lines up and down the bare skin. "When you put it on did you know I'd spend the duration of the night fantasizing about taking it off?"

Her mouth was dry so she swallowed. "I wore it because I liked it," she answered defiantly and was rewarded by a wicked gleam in his eyes.

"I like it, too," he said, before lowering his head, kissing her neck, using his tongue to create tiny circles of heat down the column to her shoulder blade.

Noelle inhaled, letting the scent of his cologne permeate her senses. His hands were barely touching her, yet his tongue was claiming her.

When his teeth latched on to the first thin gold and orange-twined strap, Noelle audibly sucked in a breath. With a torturously slow movement, he lowered the first strap. Then he surprised her by moving around her from the back, tracing kisses along the back of her shoulders, her spine, to the other shoulder. Again his teeth scraped along her skin as he slipped the second strap down. When she didn't voluntarily move her arms, he lifted them both until the straps were released, coming around to the front of her just as the top portion of the dress folded down, baring her naked breasts.

It was his turn to inhale, exhaling roughly through his parted lips. Immediately he was lowering himself, taking first one nipple into his mouth for the sweetest kiss Noelle had ever experienced, then moving to the next. To her surprise he spent no more time on her breasts but proceeded to use his teeth to pull and tug at the rest of the dress until it was pooled at her feet.

A string of curses flowed fluently from Brock's lips as he looked up at her. "Don't ever," he began then closed his lips tightly, taking another deep breath. "Ever," he began again in a voice that allowed no argument, "let me catch you out without me, wearing just a thong."

"The dress didn't allow for much more," she said, the words sounding extremely inconsequential at the moment.

He was standing by that time, taking her mouth in a rough, intimate kiss that had Noelle's arms wrapping helplessly around his neck. "Never again," he said tearing his mouth away from hers and breathing heavily. "Say it, Noelle. Never again."

She heard his words but they were swimming around in her mind, going under, then resurfacing as if caught in a whirlpool. His hands were on her bare back, sliding down to cup her buttocks, his lips still touching her skin in fiery caresses. *How the hell did he expect her to say anything?*

He kissed her again, dragging his tongue over her teeth, dipping deep into her mouth to tangle around her tongue, suckling, taking, devouring, before pulling away again.

"Say it!" he commanded, holding on to her bottom with one hand and grabbing her hair with the other, moving his fingers frantically until whatever style she'd come into the casino with was effectively ruined.

"Never," she whimpered as he pulled her head back so that she was looking up directly into his face. "Never again," she finally managed and was rewarded by yet another scolding kiss.

With a quickness she and Brock were becoming known for, Noelle was lifted into the air, then settled on the very table they'd just been playing on, cards sticking to her bare back.

Brock ripped his shirt open, popping buttons up and down his chest and violently removing the cufflinks, as he tore it off. A quick tug of his undershirt and his chest was bare. His pants, boxers and shoes were gone in a blur. Even the retrieval of a condom from his wallet and the sheathing of his impressive arousal were fast.

Noelle didn't care—she was on fire, her legs trembling, heart pounding. God, she wanted him. Fiercely. Completely.

When he stood over her, she lifted her arms to him in invitation. He paused, roped muscles in his arms tensing as he looked down at her nakedness.

"Please don't stop me, Noelle. Not now."

She heard his words, recognized them for the permission he was asking and the strength it was taking him to do so. Any other man, with the offering before him would have taken, gladly. But Brock was asking, needing, wanting.

And she was falling, fast, assuredly, in love with this man.

"Take me, Brock. Please."

When he came down lower it wasn't fast but it was hot. The closer he came, the soft touch of his lips to her temple, her cheek, her lips, was hot and sweet and just what she needed.

"Stop thinking," he whispered. "I want you mindless of anything but me. Just me, Noelle."

His tongue plunged into her mouth as if he were attempting to wash away all memory of any other man.

It was unnecessary, Noelle thought as her hands gripped the back of his head, holding him close. He was Brock and he wanted her, all of her. She knew, could feel it in his touch, see it in his eyes, know it in the way he respected her in business and in bed.

When Brock slipped into her warmth he shuddered, his body immediately embraced by hers. Lifting her thighs high in his arms he planted his feet firmly and began to ride.

It was glorious, surreal, intoxicating. This woman and the way she made him feel. He'd craved her, from that very first day he'd seen and kissed her. It had been like an addiction the way one taste had driven him crazy with need. This wasn't a part of the business plan. He wasn't supposed to fall for a woman this way. And yet there was absolutely no doubt in his mind, this woman was made for him, and he for her.

With each thrust the deal was sealed for Noelle. Good or bad she knew her mind, her heart. It had never felt this way before, her heart that is. She'd never felt this way before. Sex had been good, men had been nice, but making love had never been as sweet. Falling in love had never been as swift. Falling in love had simply never been for her.

Now she embraced it, embraced Brock and what he was doing to her. Right at this very moment he was taking her to higher heights, pushing her until she had no choice but to helplessly tumble into the abyss of sexual pleasure. By now her legs had been hoisted up on his shoulders, her palms flattened against the felt table that she was now scraping as she screamed her release.

Brock followed right after her, falling hopelessly as

her tightening thighs and heartfelt cries of ecstasy pulled his release from him with smooth efficiency. When his body finally finished shaking, his breath slowing to some semblance of order, he turned his face and kissed her ankle. Spying her shoes he pulled back slightly, holding both her ankles in his hand and looking from one gold shoe to the other.

"I don't know where you get these things or who the hell made them, but I'm eternally grateful for his genius," he said, then proceeded to kiss each ankle, down the front line of her foot to her toes.

Noelle could do nothing but sigh until he was finished and putting her legs back down. She felt weak and depleted and as if she were glowing all over. Flattening his palms on the table on either side of her head, he looked down at her with a devilish gleam in his eyes.

"You can rest up on the ride home because I'm not finished with you. I just need to get you into a bed, finally."

With those words, Brock lifted Noelle from the table and proceeded to dress her in much the same fashion as he'd undressed her—with slow precision that made her shiver.

When he was dressed and they were finally leaving the casino, Noelle stopped and hugged him.

"What was that for?" Brock asked, staring down at her quizzically.

"For winning. Again."

His smile was quick, his kiss on the tip of her nose sweet. "How could I not win with you as the prize?"

His words were so endearing that she'd almost slipped up, almost told him that she loved him. Almost.

Las Vegas, Nevada

The double doors were white with gold handles and locks. The lawn was impeccable, glittered marble lined the walkway, while two cars—a Rolls Royce and a Cadillac Escalade—sat outside the closed doors of the two-car garage.

Trent rang the bell and waited. In another ten seconds he was kicking the damn door down, his patience already worn thin.

Luckily it swung open and a woman who looked to be in her midforties with a bad gold-blond weave glared at him through icy eyes.

"Who are you and why are you banging on my door like you're the law?"

Flattening his palm on the door, Trent pushed past her, making his way into the foyer of the house. "I'm worse than the law," he said.

"Hey! You don't have any right busting into my house. I'm calling the—"

She'd slipped past Trent and was heading toward a cordless phone sitting on a white marble table just beneath a huge gold framed mirror.

"When you get the cops on the line, tell them about the blackmail scheme you and your husband cooked up against the Donovans," he said, his voice as lethal as the way he glared at her.

She stopped abruptly and spun around to face him. "Who are you?"

Trent smiled. "Today's your lucky day Mrs. Simmons. I'm Trenton Donovan."

The effect was priceless. The woman's already light complexion paled.

"I see we won't have to waste time with formalities. Maybe you'd like to change before I carry your sorry behind to the police station."

"You can't arrest me—you're not a cop," she said defiantly, her shifting eyes giving away the fact that she wasn't totally sure her words were true.

Trent chuckled. "There you're wrong. I'm an officer of the United States Armed Forces and a licensed PI in the state of Nevada. I can and *will* arrest you and take you in. I've just got two questions for you: Where are the photos, all the copies including any negatives or originals? And do you want to go to jail dressed in your robe or would you rather put on something a tad more decent?"

"Go to hell!" she screamed, and attempted to run.

She truly had no idea who she was dealing with. With two steps, Trent had her around her waist, lifting her into the air. Her arms were instantly flailing, her legs kicking wildly. So when he stomped into her living room and dropped her onto the couch, she was already out of breath.

"You've got two minutes to get yourself together and gather those photos before I tie you up and tear this house to shreds." He took a step back, lifted his arm and tapped the face of his watch.

The normally well-put-together, ready-for-anything Claudette Simmons looked as if she were two seconds away from either spitting nails or having a nervous breakdown. But it was when she was scrambling to get herself upright on the sofa that she heard the police sirens.

With a jerk of her head, she looked toward the windows, then back at Trent, who only looked down at his watch once more.

"Fine," she said through tight lips and was once again up and pushing past him.

Trent followed her through the ornately decorated house. Adam and Max had pulled Luther's financial records, along with those of the private accounts held by Claudette. One was definitely higher than the other. It seems Mrs. Simmons had been making a career of being married to Luther. The last two properties Luther had attempted to purchase had been underbid by his own wife, who had in turn sold them under an anonymous company name and pocketed the profits. In Trent's eyes her little blackmail scheme of Noelle and the Donovans was probably her last hoorah where Luther was concerned. She had enough money to drop his cheating behind like a hot potato. Trent had to chuckle at the irony.

When they were in the library Claudette moved a painting to the side and began working the dial of a pretty high-tech safe she had hidden in the wall. Trent didn't bother watching the combination. If he wanted in he'd simply blow the damn wall up. Patience wasn't one of his high points. But his eyes rested on the painting, which was now tilted at a weird angle. He'd seen it someplace before but couldn't recall where. It was nice, though, with its muted colors of a black man playing a trumpet.

"Here are your pictures," she snapped, turning back at him with an envelope in hand. When Trent snatched them from her, she folded her arms over her chest. "They weren't even in good focus so I was hoping I wouldn't have to use them."

Just to be thorough—not because he wanted to see Noelle in a compromising position because that might make his last little bit of calm fade and he'd conveniently forget his father's studious training about not hitting a female—he glanced at them. She was right—the images were really blurry, so much so that trying to pinpoint the identity of either of the parties in the picture was difficult. It probably wasn't Noelle with Luther at all. But Trent knew that, when it came to the press, the truth didn't really matter.

"I want the negatives," he said flatly.

With a roll of her eyes Claudette turned back to the safe and removed a black pouch. In the distance they both heard footsteps.

"You said if I gave you the photos there would be no police," she said, pulling the lapels of her robe closed.

"No," Trent said with a shake of his head. "I informed you that I could arrest you if need be but that I'd prefer you turn over the photos. These guys," he said, nodding toward the door at the exact moment two uniformed Las Vegas police officers entered, "are definitely here to arrest you for extortion."

"But you have the photos," she was yelling, even as the first officer came around, grabbing one of her wrists and cuffing her.

"That I do," Trent said, tapping his hand against the folder. The officer had her cuffed and was about to lead her out of the room when Trent stopped her and leaned over to whisper in her ear. "And if I so much as hear a whisper of these photos or anything else about your jackass husband and my sister, I won't hesitate to release the tape I have."

"What tape?" Claudette gasped.

Trent grinned. "I almost forgot to mention the little bit of adult entertainment in my little safe. The one with you and a certain Senator's wife performing certain… shall I say acts of a sexual nature."

Her face paled.

"Don't fret, Claudette. My tape is in excellent clarity. There will be no mistakes about who is doing what, to whom."

Her mouth opened to say something, then snapped shut as the second officer began to read her rights. Trent was still laughing when he walked out of the Simmons house. When his cell phone rang he was expecting to hear Tia's voice wondering where he was and how long he was going to be. So it was with a smile in place and a deep desire to see his fiancée that he answered the phone so cheerfully, "Trent Donovan."

"We've got trouble," Max's somber voice said on the other end, and Trent's good mood vanished.

Chapter 21

They'd showered together. A blissfully sweet half hour filled with steamy hot water, thick lather and long, luscious kisses that promised more to come.

Back in Brock's bedroom for only the second time since coming to St. Michaels Noelle stood at the end of the bed. She'd been sitting on one of the deep-cushioned chairs across the room, applying the lotion she'd retrieved from her bedroom to her body. Brock had propped up his pillows, crossed his arms over his bare chest and watched her.

Now she stood before him not having to wonder what thoughts were going through his mind, but asking just the same. "What are you thinking?"

He didn't even blink an eye. "I'm thinking about how lucky I am to have met you."

Her hands were on her hips and her fingers drummed nervously. That wasn't what she'd expected him to say. "Like you said, we probably would have met eventually." Snappy remarks were always her best defense.

"I think the timing was perfect. I think you are perfect."

She looked down. "As bodies go I guess I'm okay."

Brock got up from the bed, walking until he was standing directly in front of her. Cupping her face in his hands he said seriously, "You can't ask me to see more than just your body if you're not willing to do so yourself."

His gaze was intense, his touch electrifying, his words so very true. "Sorry. Old habit."

"One that I don't want you reverting to again. You're a terrific woman, Noelle. Smart and tenacious, caring and loyal. Any man that doesn't see that is more than a fool and not worth your time."

She nodded, feeling his declaration straight down to her toes. "I know."

"Now with that said, any man who sees you for what you really are and attempts to make a play for you is a dead man walking. Sharing is not one of my strong points."

"That's not true. You've shared so much with me since I've been here. More than I suspect you've ever shared with anyone else."

Brock sighed. "You bring out the best in me."

She smiled.

"But my word is true. I'm a very possessive man once I've staked my claim."

"Oh, really?" she asked as his hands slid from her face to her shoulders, pulling her even closer to him. "Is that what you're doing?"

"That's what I've already done."

Slipping her hands between them, Noelle gripped his erection and watched with pleasure as his eyes grew darker. "Then maybe it's time I do a little claiming of my own."

"Please," was all Brock could manage as she slid down farther, her hands stroking him harder.

Her breath touched him first, warm and teasing, fanning over the head of his arousal. Brock closed his eyes only to have them shoot open again as her mouth closed over him.

His fingers were in her hair, scraping her scalp, guiding her head over him as his hips matched the rhythm created. When he could no longer stand the sweet torture he pulled away, lifting her up into his arms, kissing her deeply as he carried her to his bed.

"This is where you belong," he said, laying her gently on top of the comforter, then reaching into the nightstand to retrieve a condom and sheathing himself before settling over her. "Now and forever." His words were muffled as he buried his face in the crook of her neck, his thick arousal into her center.

Noelle wrapped her legs and her arms around him, cradling him. They moved ever so slowly, a sharp contrast to their previous intimate interludes. It was decadent, this sweet, slow climb they were taking together. His strokes were deep, punctuated by some compliment, some promise he was making to her.

Her mind roared, wanting so desperately to share her feelings with him, yet still afraid to put herself completely out there in that way. Brock didn't seem to mind as he continued kissing her, caressing her, loving her.

And when her body finally gave up its fight, letting yet

another orgasm ripple through her with delightful ease, Noelle shuddered. Not simply at the feel of completion but on the precipice of happiness, of finally finding the love she'd been searching so long and hard for.

Having allowed her own thoughts to scare her to the point that she needed desperately to be alone to sort them out, Noelle had sneaked out of Brock's bed not long after he'd finally fallen asleep. For a moment she'd stood there and watched him, wondering how he would react to her being in love with him. Would she tell her that he couldn't offer her anything? That he was tainted with the misfortune of his parents?

She didn't know what he would say and, worse, didn't know how she'd react if he did. For the first time in Noelle's life she wasn't going to push an issue into a compartment and deal later. She was going to think on it and deal with it now. Well, in the morning when they were both well rested and thinking clearly. As she tip-toed out of his room and returned to hers, she figured she was doing the right thing. Something had definitely changed between them tonight, something too signifi-cant to put off. However, sleeping enfolded in his arms was muddling her thoughts, giving her a sense of se-curity that might not really be there. So until she was absolutely sure that this was going where she hoped it was, she would sleep in her own bed.

Alone in her room, Noelle was able to think clearly about the step forward she and Brock had just taken, until finally her mind had given up the battle and she'd slept—only to be awakened, she wasn't sure how much later, by a strong hand clamping down over her mouth.

"Luther! Are you out of your mind? What are you doing here?" Noelle whispered a second after the hand slipped from her mouth and the lamp beside her bed was switched on.

"You told me to fix the situation, so I am," he said, giving her that same smooth smile he'd had the day she'd met him. Luther was still a good-looking man, no matter how much Noelle despised him now. His pecan complexion and seductive light green eyes were the first things she'd noticed that day in the casino. She noticed them this morning, yes, it was morning, barely, she noted as the orange-red sky was just shooting dull rays of light through the blinds in her room.

"By breaking and entering?" Pulling the sheets up to her neck, she sat up in the bed.

"No. By getting us out of here. Now I've got a car waiting. You just need to get dressed and we can go."

"Go where?"

He'd been pacing back and forth, tiny beads of sweat peppering his forehead. He wore jeans and tennis shoes. That should have been the first tip off that he wasn't exactly stable at the moment. No, the fact that he'd obviously broken into Brock's house clearly stated he'd gone overboard.

"The way I see it, the only way we can get away from Claudette and her crazy scheme is to leave the country. That way even if she shows the pictures it doesn't matter because we'll be long gone."

For a moment Noelle could only stare at him.

"What?" he exclaimed. "Get out of bed and get dressed."

This fool had definitely bumped his head if he

thought for one second she was going anywhere with him. "Luther, I'm going to give you about ten seconds to get the hell out of this room, out of this house before I call the cops." Or worse, Noelle thought as their voices were steadily escalating, Brock.

Why hadn't she just stayed in his room last night? Oh, no, she'd had to try and prove another point. They were going to take their relationship slow if it was the last thing she did. Still, had she stayed wrapped safely in his arms, she wouldn't be staring at this lunatic right now.

Throwing the covers to the side she finally climbed out of bed, only to stand in front of Luther, poking her finger into his chest.

"You have lost your everlasting mind! First you lie to me and cheat on your wife. Then you harass me with a bunch of bull about wanting to leave her and be with me. Then, as if the previous actions weren't bad enough, you try to help your wife blackmail me. And now…now you bring your silly behind in here talking about running away like we're some star-crossed lovers!"

Luther had been backing up with each poke, each word she tossed at him, while Noelle's anger was steadily brewing.

"I'm not going anywhere with you, now or ever. But I will tell you what I'm going to do," she said, then reached for the first thing in her line of vision—the wire trashcan near the door. Picking it up she hauled it over her head and brought it down with a loud crack over Luther's skull.

"I'm going to beat some sense into you once and for all!"

That's the scene Brock walked in on—Noelle yelling and screaming as she cornered a man in her bedroom, beating him with, of all things, a trash can.

"What the hell?" he asked, not expecting to receive an answer. Then he took another step, snagging Noelle around the waist and spinning her in the opposite direction.

"Let me go! I'm not finished with him yet!" she yelled as he set her down a good distance from the man now sliding to the floor.

"Put that down," Brock told her. When she didn't comply, he reached for her arm and yanked the trash can from her grip.

"He deserves it for all he's put me through! I should—" her words ended abruptly as she made another dive for the man.

If he weren't facing an intruder in his house and a maniacal woman, Brock might have found the situation funny as hell. Instead, with a grip that was much sterner, much tighter than before, he moved Noelle back, pushing her onto the bed until her mouth dropped open, then clapped shut. "Stay there!" he warned her, and watched with fascination as all she did in response was huff and fold her arms over her chest.

Scrubbing a hand over his face, he turned to the intruder. "Get up!" Brock yelled at him.

"Nah, man. She's crazy. I'm not moving until you tie her up somewhere."

What? Was he in the twilight zone? Was this grown man huddled in the corner, afraid to move for fear of being attacked by Noelle?

Reaching down, Brock grabbed him by the front of

the hooded jacket he wore and hauled him up. "Who the hell are you?"

"I—I—" He was stuttering like a child who'd stolen something.

"That's Luther! With his dumb, conniving behind!" Noelle shot back.

Well, wasn't this just peachy, Brock thought, then unceremoniously let go of the hold he had on Luther's jacket, watching him stumble to stay upright.

"How did he get in here, Noelle?"

For a moment she didn't answer, then in a very clipped, very purposeful tone she said, "He broke in. How do you think he got in here?"

Brock raised his fist and brought it crashing down into Luther's jaw. The man, or the sorry excuse for a man, fell straight back against the wall, holding his face.

Not hesitating, Brock landed another blow to his nose this time and watched as blood instantly spurt into the air.

"Dammit! You broke my nose!" Luther whined as Brock gave him about a minute to touch and feel the damage to his face before hitting him with a gut blow that was designed to bring up every meal Luther had eaten since around noon the day before.

The sound he made as he crumbled to the floor was sickening and invigorating all at the same time.

"Oh, great. I missed all the action," Trent said, pushing through the bedroom door to see Brock shaking his fist and Luther Simmons balled up in the corner moaning.

Chapter 22

"Oh, honey, you should have called me and told me what was going on," Jade said, folding Noelle into a hug the minute the men were all huddled on the other side of the dining room.

The last twelve hours had been a frantic blur for Jade, from the moment she'd overheard Trent telling Linc that Luther was on his way to Maryland. She'd never dressed so quickly in her life. Linc had tried to convince her that she didn't need to come, but she wasn't trying to hear any of his excuses. She'd deal with him keeping secrets from her later.

On the plane ride she'd made Linc tell her the whole sordid tale of how Luther had involved her sister in an affair while he was still married and then had the audacity to try and blackmail her. Jade had been furious with both Linc and Noelle for not telling her any of this over the last few months.

Jade also had to learn, on the plane ride to Maryland—thank goodness they were traveling across the country or she might still be in the dark—Trent's role in this little episode.

Apparently Brock had called Trent, asking him to look into Luther's background. Well, that was right up Trent's alley, and her military-trained brother-in-law had instantly done just that. He'd also gone to see Claudette Simmons and had her arrested. News after that had led to their little trip out here. Jade was more than angry with a few members of the Donovan family, but she'd have to deal with all that later. Right now, she had to take care of Noelle.

"Jade, you shouldn't have come all the way out here. The girls need you," Noelle said, trying desperately to let go of the hurt she still felt from Brock's question. *Did he really believe she'd invited Luther to his home?* If not, then why ask her how Luther got there? Last night with Brock and the couple of days prior had been so good. She'd thought they were actually on their way to a meaningful relationship. Now, she wasn't quite sure.

"Beverly will keep the girls. And with Tia and Camille hanging around, they'll be well taken care of. You, on the other hand…" Jade shook her head. "What am I going to do with you? I knew I shouldn't have let you come out here. But I was trying to give you a chance. It was just too soon after the fiasco with Luther. Whew, I'm glad that's over with."

"Hold on," Noelle said, trying to get her thoughts straight. "What do you mean you shouldn't have let me come? Jade, I'm a grown woman. I make my own decisions."

Her sister didn't say anything, just continued brushing the sides of her hair and not looking at her.

"That's it, isn't it? You don't think I can make my own decisions? That's why you left your newborn twins to come and rescue poor little Noelle, again." She huffed then pulled out of Jade's grasp. "This was not my fault! I didn't mess up this time. Luther did."

Noelle walked across the room, waiting for Jade to say something, hoping she was wrong and that her sister was only here out of concern and not her usual protective instincts.

"I didn't say it was your fault," Jade said quietly.

Noelle sighed. "But that's exactly what you're thinking. You think because I messed up by being with Luther I created this whole situation. But I didn't, Jade."

Running her fingers through her hair, which probably looked a hot mess, Noelle glared at her sister. "I met a man. I liked him so I went out with him. We began what I thought was a relationship. Unfortunately, because he happened to be a liar and a cheat, that wasn't true. But I didn't ask for this. I didn't go looking to be used this way."

"Noelle," Jade tried to interject.

"No." Holding up her hand to silence her sister, Noelle kept right on talking. "I'm tired of everybody looking at me as if they're waiting for the other shoe to drop. You've done that all my life and it's time for it to stop. Poor Linc just picked up where you left off. While he's not as intense as you are, he still maneuvers things for me. First the job at the Gramercy, school and now this job. I can do things for myself. I can work and live and find love, all by myself."

Her heart was hammering in her chest and Noelle figured she was probably going overboard but it felt so good to be releasing all this pent-up frustration. She was actually saying the things she'd been thinking for quite some time and it was taking a tremendous load off to do so.

"I'm not perfect, so things are going to go wrong in my life the same way they do in everybody else's, but it's okay because that's normal."

By now everyone had stopped talking to stare at her. Noelle didn't give a damn—they all needed to hear it. They all needed to know that Noelle Vincent was her own woman, with her own goals and aspirations.

"I don't need to be protected or cushioned from bad things and I definitely don't need to be bailed out of every scrape I get into. For God's sake, the best lessons learned are the ones learned the hard way. If you all keep picking up the pieces, how do you ever expect me to learn? Well, it doesn't matter because despite your efforts I have learned how to be an adult and how to make adult decisions and—"

"Shhh."

Noelle felt his hands on her shoulders, stopping her next steps and her next words. It was Brock. Only his touch could soothe and quiet her at the same time.

"It's all right, baby. Nobody's going to do those things to you anymore. We know this wasn't your fault."

She was already shaking her head, denying his claim. "No, Jade doesn't know. She thinks I'm a screwup. She had to come all the way across the country to fix my mess again."

"Jade came all the way across the country because she's your sister and she loves you. She wanted to make sure you were safe."

With tear-filled eyes Noelle looked up at Jade. She was dressed in a cream-colored linen pantsuit, her auburn hair curling at her shoulders, her eyes almost identical to Noelle's misting with tears as she nodded, agreeing to what Brock had just said.

"I guess I've been mothering you for so long it's kind of hard to stop," Jade said when Linc came to wrap an arm around her.

"We all just care about you, Noelle. If it's a bit overbearing, blame it on our hearts, not our minds," Linc offered.

Brock was rubbing his hands up and down her arms now as the tears continuously flowed down her cheeks. Sure, she felt like a colossal ass for making such a scene, but she also felt relief that they all understood where she was coming from.

"Why don't I take you back upstairs so you can lay down? It's been a pretty eventful morning. I'm sure you're tired."

She wasn't really tired, not anymore. But she'd take this as a way to get Brock alone. There were some things she needed to get off her chest where he was concerned also.

"That sounds good," she said in a tiny voice, then went to Jade, hugging her and Linc. "Thanks, you guys, for everything."

"It's okay, sweetie. You can vent whenever you feel like it," Jade said.

Linc tweaked her nose. "Yeah, but keep the tears to a minimum. I'm just a man, you know."

"I'll remember that," Noelle said with a smile, then turned to walk out of the room beside Brock.

"Wow, I thought she was going to skin you both alive," Sam Desdune said from his perch on the chair in the corner of the dining room.

"Be quiet, Desdune. I'm sure your family has the same types of blowups," Trent said, thanking God Noelle hadn't turned her wrath on him. However, he knew the moment she got herself together she'd be gunning for him.

Sam was Trent's partner in D&D Investigations. He was also a good friend, so when Trent had mentioned what he was working on Sam had immediately offered his help. Trent knew that Sam was still feeling guilty for the stalker from an earlier case coming all the way to Vegas to get back at Trent through Tia. But that was water under the bridge. He had Tia and she was safe, so Trent was happy.

Sam, however, Trent wasn't so sure of. Earlier this year Sam had been engaged to Leeza Purdy, a snobby Connecticut socialite with a voice that would drive a crazy man to sanity. Two months ago, when Sam had come to Vegas to warn Trent about the stalker, he'd told him that he'd broken his engagement to Leeza, citing he just couldn't take it any longer. Trent had laughed and congratulated his friend. That, no doubt, had been a good move.

Because Sam was only a few hours away from Maryland, he'd come down to lend a hand with the Luther issue. Luckily for them all, Luther had been smart enough—in the end—to go quietly with the police officers who had arrived after Trent had found the man in Noelle's bedroom.

Brock's right hand was a little swollen and would probably hurt for the duration of the day, but he sensed it had felt good to break Luther's nose. Trent only wished he'd been the one to hit him.

"Yeah, but this is way more entertaining," Sam told him.

"There's never a dull moment where the Donovans are involved," Max added.

"So I'm going to head down to the police station just to make sure all the loose ends with Luther are tied up," Sam said, standing and stretching his long arms. Taller and leaner than the Donovans, Sam had the look of a half African-American, half Frenchman, and the Creole background to go along with the look.

"That sounds like a plan," Trent conceded. "You up for a ride, Max?"

"Nah, I was thinking more along the lines of a round of golf," he said with a grin.

Max was younger than Trent by a year. His brother Ben was a year younger than Adam. Out of all the cousins Trent, Adam and Linc were closest to Uncle Everette's children because Uncle Albert had opted to live in Texas instead of on the west coast with the rest of the clan. As far as Trent knew Max didn't have a steady woman in his life, either—something about the accident he'd had in college kept him from being with a woman on an extended basis, and since the Donovan men—until recently—weren't interested in tying themselves down with a woman, Trent had never questioned it. But it was said that once you fell in love you looked at everyone around you to fall in the same fashion. Well, Trent was wondering about Max's bachelorhood, as well.

"Golf sounds good. We can stop by the police station, finish up with Luther and then hit the course."

"Should we wait for Linc and Brock?"

Max shook his head. "I think Brock is going to be detained for a while."

Trent laughed as they all looked toward the doorway and the stairs that Brock and Noelle had climbed up just moments before. "You might be right. And Jade will probably keep Linc occupied, as well. So it looks like it's just us, fellas."

"Cool. Let's go."

Chapter 23

In the bedroom Brock attempted to pull Noelle close for a hug, but she easily pulled away.

"I'm sorry they upset you," he said, undoubtedly speaking of Linc and Jade.

"They aren't the only ones," she quipped. Her mind was simply reeling, first with her conflicting feelings about Brock, then with Luther and his fool actions and Linc and Jade's overprotectiveness, right back to Brock and her doubts where he was concerned.

"Tell me what else is bothering you," he said calmly, moving over to sit in the chair closest to the window.

"Do you trust me?" she blurted out.

Brock didn't falter. "Yes."

"Remember when I told you that, despite all my mistakes, I only sleep with one man at a time?"

"Yes."

"Did you believe me?"

"Of course I believed you."

"Then why did you ask how Luther got into my room? Did you think I let him in?" Her heart beat wildly as she waited for the answer, hoping and praying it would be what she wanted—no, what she needed—so desperately to hear.

"Baby, I asked you because I wanted you to tell me he broke in. I wanted one more excuse to whip his ass. You thought I was accusing you?"

Noelle turned away, unable to fully bask in the euphoria of his words. "I don't know what to think right now. Everything is happening so fast. A month ago I came here to work, then I met you and we…we— Things are just out of control."

His hands were on her shoulders, slipping down her arms to wrap around her, cradling her. "I know. It seems like just yesterday I was walking around this big house by myself. And then I got a call saying that a site manager was on her way. From the moment you stepped off that plane, my life's been in an uproar. Everything I thought I knew or thought I wanted has changed and you're the reason."

"That wasn't my intention," she said quietly.

"Mine, either. But we're both adults. We can handle this, baby."

He sounded so sure while Noelle still felt as if she was wavering. "What exactly is it that we're handling, Brock? I mean, just a few weeks ago you told me you had no future to offer a woman. And while it might seem like I'm game for a whirlwind affair, I'm really not. I'm tired of the back and forth of the dating game. I want a family and stability."

She felt his body tense, then just as quickly relax. "I didn't think I had anything to offer, but that was before you showed me how to love you."

Noelle turned in his arms, staring back at him in surprise. "I didn't do anything."

"Yes, you did," he said with a smile, still holding her tightly against him. "You told me exactly what you wanted and what you wouldn't tolerate. I had no choice but to get my act together. You changed me, Noelle. You gave me a reason to want to move forward with my life, to put the past behind me."

Warming inside, Noelle lifted a hand to his cheek. "You're still haunted by your past," she said sadly.

"But you'll help me with that, too, I'm sure."

Turning his head Brock kissed the inside of her palm. Noelle's eyes closed only to open up to his staring back intently. "I will help you with anything you need," she promised, and meant every word.

"Good," he said, dropping a quick sloppy kiss on her lips then releasing her.

She almost stumbled it was so abrupt.

"Now get showered and dressed. There's somewhere I want to take you."

He was already at the door when she called to him. "But I thought I was going to lie down and rest," she said, feeling like she'd been up for three days straight, the emotional strain finally catching up with her.

"We'll rest tonight," he answered.

She raised a brow.

"Afterward, we'll rest," he corrected with a wicked

gleam in his eyes. "And we'll take tomorrow off. But I just decided to do this and I want to get it done before I change my mind."

"What is it? Where are we going?"

"You'll see," was all he said before leaving.

Alone, Noelle sat on the edge of the bed, wrapping her arms around herself. She was in love with Brock Remington. She said the words aloud just to hear how sweet they sounded. Then with a startled gasp she realized something he'd just said. *You showed me how to love you.*

He loved her.

That's what he'd said, right? Was her luck in love finally changing?

Noelle had just finished talking to Karena when Brock had come to collect her. Still not telling her where they were going, the two of them left the suddenly quiet house.

"Where did everybody go?" she asked as they walked to Brock's truck.

"Linc and Jade are visiting the town and then you know since he's here he can't help but go by the Gramercy II for a look-see. Linc mentioned the other guys were going to check out the golf course while they're here."

"When are they leaving?" she asked, pulling her seat belt across her and settling into the passenger seat.

Brock closed his door and turned to her. "Anxious to be alone with me, huh?"

His smile was flirtatious, his mood light for a change. "Yeah, I can't wait," she joked. "I just don't like that all of them had to come running out here to my rescue."

He'd started the truck and was backing out of the driveway when he slammed on the brakes. "They came because they care," he said.

Noelle inhaled deeply, then released a long slow breath. "I know. I guess I'm still getting used to being in a big family after all."

"I can understand," Brock said as he continued driving, turning off his property onto the open road. "It took a little while for me to get used to."

"Do you see Albert often?" she asked, because Brock didn't talk about his adopted father much.

"Not as often as I probably should," he admitted. "I talk to him at least twice a month. Bailey calls me weekly, mothering me from afar. And Brandon and I keep close contact."

"So it's just the Donovan family as a whole that you stay away from?"

"No. It's not like that. At least, that's not the way I intended it to be. I guess I just got so used to being alone."

"You thought you deserved to be alone," she corrected.

With a glance to his right Brock couldn't help but chuckle. Would he ever get used to her candor? The answer was, his life would never be the same without it. "You're right. I used to think it was my destiny to be alone."

"But you let Kent and Josette in."

"On a limited basis. Kent is a great guy and a good friend. He and Josette are great together. They probably think I'm a serious head case after all these years."

"Nah, I think they see what I see."

"And what's that?"

"A man still carrying the pain of a child."

Drumming his fingers on the steering wheel, Brock was quiet for a few minutes. Noelle kept looking out the window as if what she'd just said was nothing more than a comment on the weather, when, in actuality, she'd just diagnosed him as easily as an experienced psychiatrist.

They drove in silence for the next forty-five minutes, Brock letting his thoughts and feelings circulate through his mind. This morning had been eye-opening for him. No, it had been skull-cracking. Seeing Noelle fighting the man who threatened her happiness had knocked down his final barriers. If this woman, who had been through so much in her young life, could keep on fighting for a happy future, so could he.

He told her he didn't speak with Albert as much as he should have and that was absolutely true. So much so that he'd called Albert right after he'd left Noelle this morning. His adoptive father had been happy to hear from him and even happier by the way Brock had finally opened up to him.

Since Brock had entered high school Albert had held the door open for him to talk about his parents, about how their situation had affected him. But Brock had declined. He'd thought he was handling the situation. In almost six weeks Noelle had knocked his blinders off. He wasn't handling it, he was running, just as he'd accused her of doing.

Things happened in Noelle's life, he knew from what Linc had told him and what Noelle had admitted to herself. Yet, everyday she awakened, giving her job, her family, her life one hundred percent of her efforts. She wanted love and happiness and she wasn't going to stop until she got it. Brock admired her for her strength, her tenacity. He loved her for the inner beauty that totally outshined her physical blessings.

It was because of Albert and Darla Donovan's unconditional love and support, because of the brother and sister who never treated him like the outsider he considered himself, because of the Donovan cousins and their friends who had flown here to help because he'd called on them, and because of one hazel-eyed temptress who'd successfully wrapped him around her finger within minutes of meeting him, Brock could turn through the wrought iron gates of the Delancie Psychiatric Center without anger or feeling the weight of the world on his shoulders.

Noelle read the words just beneath the scrolled numbers on the dark brown sign nestled between two fat, white hydrangea shrubs. The lawn was sprawling green, the sun casting a fairy-tale look to the large estate with its colonial-style white house in the center.

The driveway curved around a huge Venetian garden fountain. When Brock parked the truck, Noelle was still taking in the breathtaking scenery. She didn't hear him get out or notice that he'd come around to her door and was now holding it open for her. But as she stepped out she watched as the sunlight played across his face. His golden skin tone shone beneath its haze, his normally tight mouth was relaxed, his eyes not somber but holding a sort of release. He held his hand out to her and she happily took it, laying her head momentarily on his shoulder as they walked up the redbrick steps toward the door.

She didn't know what to expect once they were inside, having never been to a psychiatric hospital before, but she definitely hadn't expected what she experienced—the homey feel of a lavish mansion. Thick rugs lined the floors, while the walls were filled with paintings, mantels holding plants and knickknacks. An elderly woman with sienna-colored skin was first to greet them. She wore a crisp black skirt suit with a lace handkerchief stuffed cheerfully in the pocket over her left breast.

"Good afternoon. Welcome to Delancie. How may I help you?" she said in a stern but friendly voice.

Brock cleared his throat then spoke. "Good afternoon. I'm Brock Remington, here to see Tarine Remington."

The woman's smile widened as she reached out a hand to Brock. "Mr. Remington, it's such a pleasure to meet you. My name is Janet Stevens. I'm the new day manager at Delancie. I've only been here a few months but Tarine has told me so much about her son."

Brock's eyes widened. "She has?"

"Why, of course," Mrs. Stevens told him, still holding the hand he'd given her to shake. "She sits right out on that back porch with her glass of lemonade in the afternoons and talks about her little boy. I must say you're quite different from what I'd pictured," she chuckled, "even though I looked in Tarine's file, so I knew you were a thirty-one-year-old man."

"Ah, Mrs. Stevens, this is Noelle Vincent," Brock said, extending his hand for Noelle to join in on the conversation.

She'd been standing close to him but still giving him his space. Coming here was hard for him, she knew, but it was also important.

"Ms. Vincent, it's a pleasure to meet you, as well. Oh, Tarine is going to be so excited she has visitors. I'll go right up and get her now."

"Is she resting?" Brock asked before Mrs. Stevens could walk away.

"Oh, no. She's in the game room, probably beating the pants off Randall Crone in checkers again. It's her favorite game. I'll just be a minute. You two go on out to the porch. She likes it out there."

Taking Noelle's hand, Brock moved through the sitting area down a short foyer to the back porch. He'd been here before. The last time he'd visited his mother, two summers ago, they'd sat on this same porch, looking out at the same pond and white painted benches. He'd talked and she'd watched the birds. He'd asked her questions and she'd hummed a tune. He'd wept for his loss and she'd picked up her glass, sipping to quench her thirst.

A slight pain in his chest had him inhaling sharply. And then she was there, one hand on his arm, the other cupping his cheek as she came to stand in front of him.

"She talks about her son," Noelle said quietly. "She remembers you, Brock. I told you she'd remember you."

Brock clenched his teeth, the emotion too strong for him to speak.

A few minutes later, as Brock and Noelle stood hand in hand looking out at the pond, quietly they heard a small gasp behind them. Each of them turned slowly.

Tarine Remington was a tall, slim woman, the same golden brown skin as Brock's, eyes a bit lighter but just as serious as her son's. She wore a pale yellow sundress with tiny lilac flowers dancing around the hem. Wrapped around her arms was a shawl made of the finest lace. Her hair was long, going down her back in one silver-streaked braid.

Noelle felt Brock's fingers shake. She gave them a quick squeeze then released them. He took one step, a little tentative, but definitely with purpose. Tarine took a step, slow and weary. The corners of her mouth lifted slightly and Noelle felt the first tear stream down her face.

Brock closed the distance, wrapping his arms around Tarine's frail form, pulling her so close and so tight Noelle feared he might crush her. Tarine wrapped her arms around Brock, a whimper escaping her lips. Thinking they should be alone Noelle swiped at her tears and made a move toward the door.

Tarine's outstretched arm stopped her. She didn't speak but it was obvious that she wanted Noelle to take her hand. And so she did. Moving out of Brock's embrace, Tarine took her son's hand and led both him and Noelle to the large white rocking chairs on the other end of the porch.

Once in front of the chairs, she motioned for Noelle to sit in one, for Brock to sit in the one beside her, then Tarine took a seat across from them. Leaning her frail body forward, she once again took Noelle and Brock's hands, entwining them together. With hers resting on top Tarine looked up at them, tears shining in her beautiful brown eyes.

"Be. Happy," she said in almost a whisper. "I want my Brock...to be happy."

Noelle was crying full force now, and as she looked over at Brock with her own blurry eyes she saw that his broad chest was the epitome of strength, his booted feet and strong hands, all male, all power, but his lips grew into a tight line, one lone tear slipping slowing, almost fearfully, down his left cheek.

They spent the duration of the afternoon sitting on that porch, rocking in those old rocking chairs, drinking the lemonade Mrs. Stevens had brought out to them. Tarine commented on the birds, then went into a diatribe of St. Michaels history, complete with a story of star-crossed lovers thrown in.

Noelle and Brock laughed with her, asked questions about her story and for a few hours saw the world through Tarine's eyes.

And when they left, even though Tarine had stiffly hugged them both, expressing her wish that she'd had children, that she'd married, that she'd had a life outside the walls of Delancie, neither Noelle or Brock felt sad.

In the truck Brock sat perfectly still for a few minutes. When Noelle leaned over the console and touched a hand to his knee, he sighed. "She knew me. For just a short time she knew who I was."

Noelle nodded. "She loved your father fiercely, Brock. You could hear it in her voice when she talked about him. And she loved you, her special little gift of love, she'd said. You both meant the world to her. Losing him was just too much."

"Losing her was devastating," he said tightly.

"She's still here."

He nodded. "I know."

"And so am I," Noelle said quietly.

Brock turned to her then, touching a finger to her chin. "I love you."

Tears flowed freely again and Noelle almost cursed. It had been almost four years since she'd cried this much and then it had only been for Grammy. *Tears cleanse the soul. They wash away the old and make room for the new.* That's what Grammy used to say whenever Noelle would catch her crying. She'd never asked her grandmother why she cried—the smile Grammy gave her through her tears always halted her words.

"I love you, too," Noelle said, finally smiling through her own tears.

Chapter 24

"All I can say is the airlines are going to love me," Noelle said when she and Brock had returned to the house to find not only that the Donovan men had returned and Kent and Josette had stopped by, but also Karena had arrived.

"Now you know, after all that talking about Mr. Brock Remington and all your confusion about him, I just had to come and get a look for myself."

The men were out back near the pool, all huddled around the grill, arguing over the best barbeque sauces and other spices. Karena, Jade, Josette and Noelle were sitting a good distance away from them on the other side of the pool.

"I hate that I've taken everyone away from their work and their lives," Noelle said, toying with the tattered edges of her denim miniskirt.

Once they'd returned from visiting Tarine and found a full house, Brock had suggested a cookout to say thank you and to see the family off—they'd all be leaving in the morning. So Noelle had changed from her slacks and blouse to something more comfortable. The water was enticing, so she'd slipped her bikini on beneath her skirt and tank top.

Now she was stretched out on one lounge chair, with Jade occupying another, wearing a long, flowing purple and white sundress. Karena lounged next to her with her five foot two height, spiky hair and chic knee-length slip dress. Josette, wearing denim capris, flip-flops and a St. Michaels T-shirt, sat in a chair.

Karena waved Noelle's comments away. "Girl, please. I needed a break. Monica is driving me crazy."

"Monica's your oldest sister, right?" Jade asked as she reached for her glass of punch on the small table.

"Yeah, she's the boss of all bosses. I just came off an eight-week buying spree and the moment I set foot in New York she's ready to send me off again. I tell you, that woman needs to find herself a man."

Noelle laughed. "She's probably sitting somewhere saying the same thing about you."

"I doubt Monica even thinks about men." Karena sighed.

"Maybe she's into women," Noelle said thoughtfully.

Jade covered her mouth so the punch wouldn't go flying all over the place as she laughed at her sister.

Karena simply shook her head while Josette chuckled.

"What?" Noelle asked innocently.

"Only you, Noelle. Only you." Karena smiled.

"Hey, no giggling over here," Sam said, walking

toward them with Max and Trent, each holding a bottled beer.

Sam was more than a little cute, Noelle thought. She'd first met him a few months ago when he'd come to Vegas to assist Trent with Tia's stalker. And here he was again. If she didn't know better, she'd think he was another member of the family.

"Are we going to eat sometime today or do the masters of the universe need more time to contemplate recipes?" Noelle asked sweetly just as Brock and Linc joined them. Brock made his way through everyone until he was sitting at the foot of Noelle's lounge chair.

He'd changed his clothes to so that he now wore shorts and a T-shirt, his Timberland boots replaced by running shoes. Damn, he was still sexy.

"The steaks will be done in about ten minutes. Max over there tried his hand at a salad." Brock was talking as he lifted one of Noelle's feet, surveying the shoes she wore—dark brown jeweled sandals with leather straps that criss-crossed all the way up to her knees.

"Forget it, Brock. She's addicted and there's no amount of therapy that can help her," Jade said, getting up to let Linc sit down, then making herself comfortable on his lap.

Everyone laughed and Noelle felt more contented then she ever had in all her life. She was surrounded by people she loved and who loved her. If she never had another happy day in her life, this one would suffice.

"So I guess I owe you guys a congratulations," Linc broke through the laughter. "The Gramercy II looks great. I know that's because of your efforts," he said, nodding toward first Josette and Kent, who had come to sit on the arm of the chair next to his wife, then to Noelle and Brock, who had placed her jewel-clad feet on his lap.

"Thanks, man. I told you it would be spectacular," Brock said.

"I never doubted you for a minute," Linc quipped.

Noelle chuckled. "Yeah, right. That's why we both received a million phone calls and e-mails and text messages."

"That's all right. We'll be more than ready for the grand opening on Labor Day. And I want all of us to be here. So, Trent, you and Tia either get married in the next four weeks or wait until after the holiday. Sam, clear your schedule. Max, you and Adam work your traveling and real estate buying around that day. And you, Ms. Lakefield, the new addition to the bunch, you take a few days off from the museum to come and celebrate with us."

"Sounds like one hell of a party." Karena smiled. "I wouldn't miss it for the world."

"So now that the Gramercy II is finished, Noelle can come back home with us in the morning," Jade said, looking tentatively from Brock to Noelle.

"I was thinking," Brock began, his hands still moving over Noelle's calves, his eyes lifting to find hers. "That maybe Noelle might consider staying here in St. Michaels for just a little while longer."

Noelle's heart lurched, her smile spread. Yes, she was definitely happy. She'd come here to do a job and she'd found the love of her life. She looked at Jade then at Karena and wondered what both these women who were so close to her were thinking at this very moment. What reckless and irresponsible thing did they think she was going to do next? And then she looked at Brock and in his eyes saw the woman he believed her to be. She saw the strength, the courage, the ambition and felt free and reborn. Tears welled in her eyes once more but she willed them not to fall.

"I was thinking," she said, sitting up and taking Brock's face in her hands, "that maybe, Brock wouldn't mind me staying here in St. Michaels for just a little while longer."

His initial answer was a kiss.

"I was thinking," he whispered against her lips, "that maybe Noelle would like to leave St. Michaels for a little while, say, go on a cruise." The birthday gift from Kent and Josette that he hadn't wanted before, was now coming in handy.

Her answer was a smile followed by another kiss. First a quick peck, then a slow nip and finally a deep intertwining, that should effectively silence whatever any of the people standing around them were thinking.

Epilogue

Karena took her seat on the plane and immediately buttoned her seat belt, just like when she got into a car. It was just one of those things she was anal about. Actually, if her sisters were the ones telling it, they'd say she was anal about just about everything. She, however, liked to think of it as having an orderly life—everything in its place and all that.

That's how she managed her business dealings, her family issues and her personal life—otherwise, she would have checked into the sanitarium by now.

She was just about to reach into her bag and pull out her laptop when the seat beside her was taken.

"Hello, again," Sam said with an easy smile that had Karena's toes warming.

"Well, hello to you. I didn't know we were booked on the same flight."

"Neither did I. Originally I was going to stay another day just to make sure that things went smoothly with Luther's extradition. But Brock assured me that he'd go down to the police station to personally see the man off." With that Sam had packed his overnight bag and headed for the airport, hoping to find a flight leaving for New York sooner rather than later. And lady luck seemed to be on his side—in more ways than one, he noted, as he was now looking into the cheerfully pretty face of Karena Lakefield.

They'd officially met last night at dinner, the one where Brock announced that Noelle would be moving to the east coast with him and Jade nearly fell out of her chair. The memory had Sam chuckling. He'd known Trent Donovan for almost ten years, and he'd shared some of the Donovan family dinners and enjoyed them immensely, but none as much as last night's.

The lady with the coal-black hair styled in a short spiky do and seductive eyes was the cause for that.

She was one of the Lakefields of Manhattan. The minute Noelle had said her name, he'd made the connection. The Lakefields ran the most exclusive and affluent African-American-owned art galleries in the United States. And although his brother-in-law, Lorenzo Bennett, had just recently opened his own gallery, Renny had nothing on the Lakefields' status in the art world.

That's exactly the impression Karena gave him— refined, delicate, priceless, a piece of art worth buying for whatever amount was asked.

"Good. I'm glad that whole episode is over. I feel so bad for Noelle and all that she's been through."

"Yeah, but she's got Brock now, so I'm sure she'll be well taken care of from here on out."

"Hmph, must be nice," she said with a frown, then looked out the window.

The plane was just about to take off when Karena's cell phone chimed. She cursed and answered it quickly, looking around to make sure none of the flight attendants noticed that she hadn't turned it off as they'd asked.

"Hello?" she whispered.

"What? Monica, I'm on the plane. Can this wait until I get home? No, I don't leave for Texas for another two weeks.

"It'll be fine if we wait, Monica. Yes. I know." She rolled her eyes skyward and sucked in a breath as the plane lifted from the ground. The worst parts of flying were takeoff and landing in her book.

"I know, Monica. Look, I'm hanging up. I'll call you when I get home.

"Okay." She sighed. "I'll call you when we land."

"Trouble on the home front?" Sam asked when she'd snapped the phone closed, turned it off and stuffed it into her purse.

"Not exactly. My older sister, Monica, is a slave driver."

"Really?"

"Yeah, she manages our family gallery in Manhattan while I do all the buying and supervise the sales division."

"I see, a family business. I know all about those."

"Are you in a family business?"

"Nah, I'm one of the apples that fell far from the tree." He chuckled. "My family owns restaurants up and down the eastern seaboard. But at my PI firm I employ mostly family members. My twin sister and Trent's cousin to name a few."

"That's right, you and Trent are good friends. Well, I'll tell you people are constantly telling me to get a life, but Monica is the one that needs to take a chill pill," Karena said with a grin.

"Really? That's interesting," Sam said thoughtfully. "How so?"

"Is Monica involved with anyone right now?"

"No. Didn't you hear when I said she was a workaholic? The only way she could be involved is if she's sneaking a man into the museum after hours because, I swear, that girl sleeps there."

"I think I know somebody who would get along famously with her."

Karena frowned. "I don't usually do the matchmaking thing," she began, "but tell me about him anyway." She was smiling and turning sideways to look at him.

"He's my brother-in-law's older brother. His name's Alex Bennett, and I don't think he ever peels himself away from his desk, either."

So as the plane soared higher into the clouds Sam and Karena talked about Alex and Monica, then about their jobs and finally about themselves. By the time the plane landed, they'd exchanged all contact information with a promise to call when they had some free time.

A promise Sam happily planned to keep.

REQUEST YOUR FREE BOOKS!

2 FREE NOVELS
PLUS 2 *FREE GIFTS!*

KIMANI ROMANCE ™

Love's ultimate destination!

KROM09

HELP CELEBRATE
ARABESQUE'S
15TH ANNIVERSARY!

2009 marks Arabesque's
15th anniversary!

Help us celebrate by telling us about your most special memories and moments with Arabesque books. Entries will be judged by the Arabesque Anniversary Committee based on which are the most touching and well written. Fifteen lucky winners will receive as a prize a full-grain leather duffel bag with the Arabesque anniversary logo.

How to Enter: To enter, hand-print (or type) on an 8 ½" x 11" plain piece of paper your full name, mailing address, telephone number and a description of your most special memories and moments with Arabesque books (in two hundred [200] words or less) and send it to "Arabesque 15th Anniversary Contest 20901"—in the U.S.: Kimani Press, 233 Broadway, Suite 1001, New York, NY 10279, or in Canada: 225 Duncan Mill Road, Don Mills, ON M3B 3K9. No other method of entry will be accepted. The contest begins on July 1, 2009, and ends on December 31, 2009. Entries must be postmarked by December 31, 2009, and received by January 8, 2010. A copy of these Official Rules is available online at www.myspace.com/kimanipress, or to obtain a copy of these Official Rules (prior to November 30, 2009), send a self-addressed, stamped envelope (postage not required from residents of VT) to "Arabesque 15th Anniversary Contest 20901 Rules," 225 Duncan Mill Road, Don Mills, ON M3B 3K9. Limit one (1) entry per person. If more than one (1) entry is received from the same person, only the first eligible entry submitted will be considered. By entering the contest, entrants agree to be bound by these Official Rules and the decisions of Harlequin Enterprises Limited (the "Sponsor"), which are final and binding.

NO PURCHASE NECESSARY. Open to legal residents of U.S. and Canada (except Quebec) who have reached the age of majority at time of entry. Void where prohibited by law. Approximate retail value of each prize: $131.00 (USD).

VISIT **WWW.MYSPACE.COM/KIMANIPRESS**
FOR THE COMPLETE OFFICIAL RULES

KP15ARACONTEST